Club Sixxes

ANOTHER PRETTY FACE

WENDI ZWADUK

ENTWINED PUBLISHING

Another Pretty Face
ISBN # 978-1-80250-246-6
©Copyright Wendi Zwaduk 2025
Cover Art by Kelly Martin ©Copyright April 2025
Interior text design by Entwined Publishing
Published by Entice, an Entwined Publishing imprint

Published in 2025 by Entwined Publishing, United Kingdom.

Entwined Publishing is a division of Totally Entwined Group Limited.

Single Books
Learning How to Bend
Must Be Doing Something Right
My Immortal
You'll Think of Me
Tangled Up
Careless Whisper
Please Remember Me
What Might Have Been
Ever Fallen In Love
Someone Like You
Love Remembers
When You're With Me
Sunshine of Your Love
Firelit Magic
Her Man
My Favorite Mistake
Silk and Decadence
Bound by Desire
Tying One On
Still the One
Play to Him
Honey and Decadence
Taken In
A Sinful Tune
Just You and Me

Love Lessons
Drawn Together
Written Together
Together Again
Dancing Together

The Refuge
Running with the Wicked
Resisting the Wicked
Serving the Wicked

Club Sixxes
Another Pretty Face

Clandestine Classics
The Phantom of the Opera

Anthologies
Treble: Savin' Me
Boots, Chaps and Cowboy Hats: Between Us

Collections
Naughty or Nice?: Wrapped in Red and Green
Heart Attack: Over My Head
Haunted By You: Miss Me Baby
Wanton Witches: Candlelit Magic
Jolly Rogered: Ruined by the Pirate
Hot Bite: Summer Sizzle
Falsely, Madly, Deeply: From Fake to Forever

ANOTHER PRETTY FACE

Dedication

For KC, TPZ

Chapter One

"All I want to do is dance." Darinda finished dusting blush and glitter across her cheeks. She checked her look in the mirror and pursed her lips.

She wanted to be strong and independent like her friends and when she visited the clubs, she could be. The woman in front of the mirror wasn't as strong. She worried about money and getting her bills paid. When she entered the dance floor or the BDSM venue, she could be anything she wanted. Money wasn't important. Bills didn't matter. She could lose herself in the music and moment. The thrill of being on display and the painful pleasure washed away her internal strife.

Not that she'd tell anyone about her problems. No one cared.

She glanced at her phone and sighed. The one thing she wanted more than to dance was to hear about her job. The accounting department at the big box store had let go of most of the secretaries due to staffing issues.

Why have a secretary when the accountants could answer their own phones?

She'd put in applications at other places and hoped she'd hear from someone soon.

Her phone beeped with an incoming text. Chloe. Not the messenger she wanted, but she'd live. She tapped to retrieve the text.

Got you an interview at the law office. just secretary work. Thurs @ 9 am.

She practically whooped. An interview. *Finally.* Her heart hammered. At the law office...the *Reid* office? Holy shit. Few were granted replies on applications, let alone interviews.

She leaned on the counter and put the phone down. The Reid Law Firm was her dream employer. Nick and Nathan Reid were not only powerful and rich beyond measure, but drop dead gorgeous. They paid well and rarely let go of staff. She'd have security for the first time in her life. What a thought. Plus, Nick and Nathan seemed to respect their employees. Not that she'd land them. She'd never get the chance to be with them, but at least she could work for them, hopefully. It was something, which was better than nothing.

She didn't have the job yet, but she needed to celebrate. Good thing she'd planned on visiting the club.

Sixxes wasn't the average dance joint. It wasn't even a club anyone could visit. Sixxes catered to the S&M crowd. Masters and their subs went the facility to live out their every naughty dream and desire. She liked visiting because she could sate her voyeuristic tendencies and play with her friends. Gavin had been training as a full master and loved using her as his showcase sub. He claimed she was the prettiest woman there. She begged to differ, but it wasn't worth arguing.

Sixxes offered her the chance to cut loose, grind on the dance floor and eventually play—mostly with Gavin. No one else had asked her to sub for them. God, she loved to sub and wanted a man who could handle her.

Another text popped onto the screen and she gritted her teeth. She had to answer Chloe before she handled the next message. She tapped out a reply.

Will be there. Thank you so much. Love you!

Once she sent that message, she checked the other. A text from Gavin.

Need to show you off. Got a big chance tonight. They want to see me in action. Wear that bondage dress we bought.

She frowned, then massaged her forehead. The bondage dress? The one made of straps? She loved that garment, but it was more strap than dress and showed off every one of her assets, with full access.

She shook her head. If he wanted her to wear it, she would, but she'd need a trench coat to cover herself in the rideshare.

The idea that she'd be on display sent instant electricity through her veins. Men would ogle her and women would want to be her. She could hear her mother's voice in her mind. *You should be ashamed of yourself. Where is your modesty?* But modesty never got her attention. It'd gotten her ignored.

Yes, sir.

He wasn't her sir, but they'd used the terminology a few times simply to signify she'd gotten the message. She abandoned her phone on the counter and padded nude to the closet. Without bothering to don panties or stockings, she shimmied into the harness dress. The straps cupped her breasts and the ones around her waist cinched her in. The sheer panel covered her outer hips, but left her pussy and the cleft of her ass completely exposed.

Blood coursed through her body and she plucked her nipples. Good God, she wanted to be touched by a man. Not just any man. A certain one — no, two — were on her mind. Nick and Nathan Reid. She longed to have them notice her. To have them touch her. Caress her. Spank her.

Fuck. She had a dirty mind and wanted them to do every dirty thing to her. She'd willingly submit to them. Have them both fill her body.

Her skin prickled and nipples beaded. She'd never see them, but the sooner she got to the club, the faster she could get to dancing and playing. She could lose herself in the fun of the play and imagine Nick and Nathan were the ones mastering her.

She fluffed her hair, then checked her makeup before stepping into a pair of sky-high pumps. She loved the way the shoes made her legs look and the power she elicited from wearing the spiked heels.

When she picked up the trench coat, she centered herself. Wearing the harness dress and heels were more like career wear. Going to the club was her job for now. Show off for Gavin, help him get his position as master, and dance. Make people happy. No one knew her at the club. No one cared that she let go that way.

She slipped the coat over her shoulders, then tied the belt. After checking she had her phone and credit card, she left her apartment and locked up behind her. She made her way downstairs to the rideshare.

When she went to the clubs, she always requested the same driver. She trusted few people and never gave Kal much information, but he got her to her destinations and never asked many questions.

The black Lexus pulled up and she nodded to Kal, then climbed into the backseat.

"Good night tonight?" Kal asked. "Going to have fun?"

"I am." She smoothed the front of her coat. Wearing so little under the coat energized her. Kal would never know that she wasn't dressed in something less revealing. It wasn't his business, though. "I'm excited." The future was wide open and she wanted to live it.

"I'm glad. I like seeing you smile." He drove across town without saying anything else and in twenty minutes, deposited her at the private entrance to Sixxes.

She winked and waved to him, then left the car and headed into the building. Her phone pinged as the ride was paid for, including the tip. The beauty of knowing the owners of the club, working with Gavin and being a regular meant she could use the private entrance instead of the public-facing doors.

The thrum of the music vibrated in her body. Excitement filled her veins. She shrugged out of her coat at the check counter and handed over her keys and phone to the attendant.

"Master G is waiting for you," the girl said. "Go to the dance floor."

"Thanks, Candy." She wished she had pockets and ready cash on her so she could tip the attendant, but the outfit didn't leave much room for storage.

"No sweat." Candy grinned, then took the coat and Darinda's belongings to the rack.

Darinda smoothed her hands over her hips, then let the rhythm of the music guide her into the dance hall. She gyrated to the music and let her inhibitions go. As she danced, she ignored the people watching her. Her body mattered. Her reactions did, too. As she brushed her hands over her chest, her nipples beaded and her pussy creamed. She flipped her hair over her shoulder, then switched time to the new song.

Gavin danced up to her. He grasped her hand and led her to the edge of the floor. "You've got lots of attention."

"I don't care." She focused on him. The wild thrill of the night overtook her. "How do you want to play?"

His eyes sparkled. "Spanking, bondage, cuffs, a vibe...and you on display. Do you wish to play with me?"

Christ, she did. "Gonna lead me around?" She loved when he did that.

"You bet." He produced a leather collar and leash from his pocket and a set of metal cuffs from his belt. "Ready?"

She offered her wrists. "I am, sir. My word is 'ghost'."

"Use it at any time." He snapped the cuffs around her wrists, then the collar around her neck. He didn't click the cuffs together, giving her time to adjust her position. "You're beautiful. I can't wait to show you off. You're making me look so good. A better Dom."

"That's what I do." She laced her hands together behind her back and allowed him to lead her by the collar and leash. The throbbing music continued, but was dulled but the change of room. The thick carpet absorbed most of the sound. The lighting changed, from bright strobes and flashes to something more mellow and soft. She forced her gaze to the floor, but hazarded glances at the audience. When he led her around the room, she noticed a few of the spectators. Some she knew, but a couple she didn't. She spotted a man on the armchair, sprawled on the thick furniture. He balled one fist, but left the other flat on the arm of the chair. His diamond ring on his right hand caught her attention. Few people who came to the club flaunted their wealth like that.

She caught sight of his face, but only for a moment. The hunger in his eyes was hard to mistake. For her? She wished. If she didn't know better, she would've sworn he was Nathan Reid, but why would someone that obscenely rich be at Sixxes?

He wouldn't.

Still, for a split second, she let her thoughts and fantasies run wild. She swore she'd have heard the gossip if the brothers were in the club. She'd never heard their names mentioned, but maybe they'd paid for extra secrecy? It was possible.

Not probable, but possible.

Gavin stopped at the St. Andrew's cross and tugged on the leash. "Girl?"

She knew what to do.

Showtime.

Nathan hadn't expected to see much when he decided to visit Sixxes. He'd been to the club a few times and liked the subs he'd seen, but no one had really stoked his pleasure.

Until today.

He flexed his hands on the arms of the chair and watched the beautiful blonde. Fucking hell, she was perfect. Slender, buxom, submissive, but he detected an independent streak within her. He longed to have that crimson mouth around his cock, to watch her on her knees. He'd bet she gave great head. She'd be gorgeous as she looked up to him with her mouth full.

Fuck, he needed to taste her.

Soon.

The Dom led the woman to the cross and released the D-ring holding the cuffs together, then affixed the cuffs around her wrists to the clips at the ends of the cross. He cuffed her ankles to the bottom, spreading her legs. The dress exposed her bare ass.

Seeing her backside made Nathan's mouth water. Such a smooth, perfect ass. The kind made for spanking. For the red streaks of his crop and hand across her skin. He caressed the bulge in his pants. The desire for her increased. He needed to know her name. Needed to possess her.

He'd never lost his head for anyone like this before. He even wanted to bring his brother in and show this woman off. He'd never spoken to her, but he craved her.

The Dom unbuckled the back of the dress, allowing the sides of the garment to droop open out of the way. He produced a flogger and whipped the tails through the air before bringing the implement down on her ass. "How many?"

She grunted and shivered, then moaned. "One. Thank you, sir, may I have another?"

"Good girl." He brought the flogger down three more times, leaving red lines on her ass.

Nathan paid close attention and watched her pussy. The telltale signs of her pleasure glittered. He loved when the sub got off on being spanked.

"Two, three, four, sir. Thank you, sir. May I have another?" she managed. She flexed her hands in the cuffs.

"Good." The Dom switched from the flogger to a crop. He peppered her backside and the lower curve of her ass with the flat leather. The sound echoed in the room. The red on her butt blossomed deeper and Nathan swore he noticed goose pimples.

Was she cold? Or that excited?

The Dom stopped spanking her. "My girl likes being spanked? Likes being on display?"

"Yes, sir." She flexed her hands again. "I deserve more. May I have another?"

"Not yet." He tucked the crop under his arm, then unclipped her cuffs. Once he'd temporarily freed her, he turned her around to face the crowd. Bright light shone on her.

Nathan doubted she could see him through the spotlight. Not such a bad thing. He needed time to research her. Wanting her was one thing, but knowing her was another. He needed to be sure of her identity. Sure she wasn't seeking his money or status. He'd been with a few women like that and wasn't in the mood to play games any longer.

The sub notched her chin, not looking at the crowd, but rather seeming to focus on the pain and pleasure coursing through her body from the spanks. She didn't move as the Dom unfastened the top of her dress, leaving her fully exposed from the waist up.

The Dom snapped his fingers and another sub scurried into the spotlight. The house sub knelt at the restrained sub's feet. He remembered the house sub from working the cloak room once before.

"You know what to do." He snapped his fingers again and the brunette produced a vibrator. While the sub vibed the blonde, the Dom first brushed the tails of the flogger over her breasts, then added a few swats.

The spanks were more noise than pain. A show for the audience.

The show worked for Nathan. He loved watching the blonde. She captivated him. As she whimpered and struggled lightly in the cuffs, Nathan noticed the pleasure spreading over her face.

"Don't you come until I give you permission." The Dom flogged her again, causing her hair to flutter with each movement. "Come when I tell you."

The blonde squirmed and panted. Her hands twitched as she balled and unballed them. She didn't beg for release, but rather followed the Dom's lead. She had spunk, but knew how to take commands.

Nathan rubbed the bulge in his pants. He wasn't about to masturbate to her yet. He'd do that later, but right now, he'd memorize every second of this scene and play it out in his mind when he got home.

He needed to meet this woman. To talk to her and introduce her to his brother. If she could handle them both, then she'd be perfect. The obedience and sweetness emulating from her spoke to him. So did that streak of adventure.

She squirmed more and tensed within the cuffs. The skin on her chest and breasts was stained pink from the flogger, giving her a rosy appearance. Bliss filled her eyes and she teetered right on the edge of climax. The more she squirmed, the more the house sub pressed the vibe to her pussy.

"Going to come?" the Dom asked. "Close?" He tucked the flogger under his arm.

The blonde groaned and struggled. "Yes, sir. May I come, sir? Please?"

"Need to?" the Dom asked. He curled his fingers under her chin. "Look at me."

She did as she was told and parted her lips. The desire and craving were palpable in the room. Nathan wanted to push the Dom aside and give her release. He needed to spirit her away from the club to his own penthouse. She wasn't meant to be owned, but rather to be pampered and cherished. Covered in jewels and silk, then spanked and fucked until she cried out. He needed to be with her. To protect her.

"Come for me," the Dom said, and pinched one of her nipples.

She screamed as she climaxed. She pulled forward in the cuffs, sagging with release. Cream slid down her thigh and glittered on her skin. "Thank you, sir," she managed. "Thank you."

The house sub withdrew the vibrator and left the scene. The Dom slid one arm around the blonde as he unlocked the cuffs. She wobbled into his embrace. He scooped her up, then carried her languid body out of the spotlight.

Nathan watched them as long as he could, careful not to draw attention to himself. He loved being at the club, but wasn't a fan of being outed. The moment anyone knew he was there, beyond the ones he trusted, was the moment people expected things from him.

Right now, he wasn't about to give anyone else pleasure. Not until he learned the name of the blonde.

Once the attention shifted to another Dom and sub in the side spotlight, Nathan left his seat. Approaching the woman tonight would be too forward. He liked to learn everything he could about his potential partners, then make a move. Not the best for romance or spontaneity, but he didn't care. Nick tended to move on instinct. Nathan planned.

Nathan walked stiffly to the desk. Colton, the owner, owed him a favor or two.

Colton stood in the doorway to his office. "Mr. Reid. I trust you're having a fun evening."

"I am." He shoved his hands into his pockets to hide the tent in the front of his pants. "I have a question and you're uniquely suited to answer it."

"I will do my best." Colton clasped his hands together. "Did you see something you liked?"

"Someone." He focused on Colton. "The main scene just a little bit ago. Blonde, brunette and the Dom."

"Yes." Colton nodded. "What about them? The brunette is Laurel. Sweet girl. Obedient. She's available tonight."

Ah, not what he wanted. "House sub."

"She is, yes." Colton laughed. "You act like you've met her before. She's not your type, so who do you want?"

"I'm inquiring about the blonde." He tipped his head to meet Colton's gaze. "She strikes me as a club girl, but not a party girl."

"Yes." Colton nodded again. "That's Darinda. She's not the typical party girl. She doesn't tend to go home with anyone."

"Is she paired up with the Dom?" He needed to know.

"No. He's a friend. In fact, the scene tonight was a showcase for the other Doms, for him to prove he's ready to be a club Dom. That was for the audience, and to get him a more permanent position here at Sixxes."

"Ah." That made more sense. No sex because that wasn't the point—no, it was to titillate the audience.

"Her name is Darinda Mace, and she's a frequent client. She dances, turns the men on, then leaves them wanting. I don't know who she's trying to attract because she does them all, but she doesn't seem affected. Like she just wants to dance and have fun.

She's a good sub, but hasn't been claimed." Colton paused. "Do you want to claim her?"

"I'd like to get to know her."

"I hope you do. She's your kind of woman—unassuming, sweet, sexy as fuck and independent," Colton said. "Want me to pass along that you're interested?"

"No." He'd said it nearly too fast and curt, but he didn't care. Once he properly met her, he'd be delicate. "Thank you."

"Any time." Colton grinned. "Have a good night."

"I will." Nathan turned on his heel and headed for the car. He'd never forget Darinda. She'd captivated him. He wanted to make love to her and hear her cry out in the same way.

Once he reached the car, he pulled out his phone and called Nick. Instead of getting his brother, he got his voicemail. *Ass.* He rolled his eyes. "I found someone. She's just who we're looking for. Forget about Suzy. I'm heading to the penthouse. We've got to talk. I've met our future." He hung up and slipped behind the wheel of the car.

Darinda Mace. Her name sounded familiar and he swiped through his phone to the list of candidates to be considered for positions at the law firm. He and Nick were looking for secretaries and general office clerks. He scanned through the names his personal secretary, Gert, had given him earlier that day. She'd be doing the interviewing, not him, but the second he saw Darinda Mace's name on the list, he pounced.

The cosmos wanted Darinda in his path. It had to be a sign.

He sent a message to Gert, instructing her to hire Darinda and that he'd explain later. He didn't owe Gert the explanation. She'd been brought on to do what he and Nick expected without question.

A reply came back in seconds.

I'll add her to the hires list, but you owe me a raise. Another one.

He snorted. If he gave Gert every raise she asked for, she'd be making as much as he and Nick did. *Not happening.* He paid her well and hadn't thought she'd reply tonight. She wasn't on the clock and the request could wait until Monday.

First, he had to do some research on Darinda, then find a way to run into her again. Something about Darinda spoke to him and he wasn't about to give up.

Not now.

Maybe not ever.

Chapter Two

Darinda picked up her trench coat and stopped at the mirror in her apartment. The last three days had been murder and she wanted them all to go away. First, getting laid off because there were too many workers in the office. She was there to file papers and thought her position was secure. It sucked not having a job, but she'd scrimped and saved enough that she'd be able to get by until something else came along.

Not a big deal.

Until her parents called.

Did she have money for them? Anything? Most people probably wouldn't mind slipping a few bucks to their parents. It wasn't a huge thing. But most people didn't have *her* parents. Her mother and father wanted cash. Lots of it. They wanted her to work for it, but for them to have the spoils. She should support them. She never did understand why. Her parents could work, they simply chose not to.

And they chose to put the weight on her back to support them.

Right now, she couldn't.

She smoothed her hands over her sheer dress. She wore a thong beneath the dress, but nothing else. Tonight, she wanted to feel sexy and forget her problems. Forget all about people wanting money, her lack of job…and not speaking to the sexy mystery man from Sixxes.

She'd never get him out of her mind.

Holy hell. The man oozed sex and command. Gavin thought he had a strong grasp of domination, but he had nothing on this guy. Perfectly tailored clothes, steely look in his eyes, the expensive haircut…he sure looked one hell of a lot like Nathan Reid.

Her body warmed all over. Nathan and his brother Nick were the stuff of her naughtiest fantasies. She wanted their hands on her body. Kissing her. Touching her. Being between them. Her nipples beaded all over again and heat surged between her legs. She pressed her knees together.

Fucking hell. She needed sex and fast, but not from just any man. The ones she wanted weren't available.

At least she'd have the chance to work for them.

Maybe she'd catch their eye while at the firm.

She snorted. What a pipe dream.

Her phone rang and she checked the screen.

Gavin.

Her shoulders slumped. *God damn.* She picked up the phone and answered. "I don't want to sub for you tonight." If she was going to sub for anyone, she wanted two specific men, who weren't available.

"Wow," Gavin said. "Aren't you feeling snippy?"

"I'm broke, my parents want money and I've got an interview in three days, but until then I'm stuck in limbo. Unless you've got a way for me to make a few bucks that's not sex or letting some scumbag feel me up, I'm not in the mood." She stepped into her knee-high boots. "I'm going to the clubs to dance. Just dance."

"I thought you might be and wanted to give you a ride. I do owe you for Friday," he said. "I got an invitation to Exposure and wanted you to come along."

"Exposure?" Only the most exclusive dance club in the area. "That's invitation only."

"I know."

"How? And why me?"

"I'll tell you when I pick you up. Wear something sexy, the sexier the better, and pearls. You always look fantastic and elegant in pearls."

She sank onto the bed and bit back a snort. "Okay." She had pearls, no problem. "When are you coming over?"

"I'm downstairs. I called off your driver and paid him for the trouble," Gavin said. "You were right—I owe you."

"Ah." No Kal tonight. Oh well. Some days, he felt like her only friend. "I'll be down in five minutes."

"Hurry your ass up."

The call disconnected. She dropped the phone, then rummaged through her jewelry box for the faux pearls. Gavin knew damn well she didn't have real ones. She draped the necklace around her throat, then fluffed her hair before pinching her cheeks to add a bit of blush.

She'd never make beauty queen, but she had confidence in her looks. She grabbed the coat, her phone and keys, then headed for the door.

Most anyone else would be hesitant to leave the apartment in an outfit so revealing. Not her. She wanted to grab attention tonight. No one noticed her any other time, but damn it, they'd see her tonight. She'd dance, have fun and enjoy herself.

When she reached the car, she'd donned the coat. Gavin waited by the vehicle and grinned. "Look at you, sexy girl." He opened the door for her.

"Hi." She swept into the passenger seat.

When he joined her on the driver's side, he sighed. "I got the gig at Sixxes."

"You did?" She clapped him on the shoulder. "That's great."

"They liked how I handled you and how I made you look good." He switched on the engine. "They also liked that my mastery and your submission got one of the bigger clients of the club interested."

"Oh?" She rolled her eyes. "Who is she?"

"I don't know the client, just that we did good and enticed them to come back." He drove away from the building. "So you've got an interview?"

"With the Reid Law Firm." She folded her arms. "I don't have a lot of hope I'll get it, but the money would be good."

"You'll be fine." He drove across town to the outskirts of town. "You always land on your feet."

"Most of the time." She'd never told him about her life before coming to the area. She hadn't wanted to. He'd look down on her. He'd call her names and lose respect. She didn't need that now.

He pulled into the parking garage next to the building. "We've got VIP access, but you have to wear a mask."

"Just me?" She frowned as he handed her the ruby-beaded mask guaranteed to obscure the view of her eyes, nose and most of her cheeks.

"Everyone." He donned a black version of her mask. "It's the theme of the night. I don't know if it's a Monday thing, or just tonight, or what."

"Ah." She left the car and stood beside the vehicle. "Do you need me to do anything special tonight?"

He offered his arm. "Dance tonight and forget your troubles. I won't leave without you."

"Thanks." She shrugged out of her coat, then abandoned her phone on the pile on the seat. "How do I look?"

His brows rose and he whistled. "Like a million bucks. Girl, you've always been beautiful, but you're a knockout now."

"You're too kind." She walked with him into the club and the thrum of the music, along with the fearlessness of being nearly nude spurred her on. She let go of Gavin and disappeared into the crowd. No one would know who she was and she could dance. She moved to the music, gyrating and losing herself in the heavy bass. As people brushed against her, she whimpered, not that anyone could hear her. Dancing was her release. Her chance to just be and live in the moment. Nothing else mattered except having a good time.

She danced and watched the crowd. A man grabbed her attention. She couldn't see his face, but the body reminded her of the man from Sixxes. Was he there, too?

Darinda grabbed a bottle of water from the bar, then downed most of the drink before heading back into the crowd to dance. She moved and twirled to the music, losing herself in the beat again. The scent of cologne wrapped around her. She'd never smelled anything so intoxicating in her life.

When she turned, another man stepped up to her. Not the sexy cologne one. This one gave her an odd feeling.

He held on to her waist and pulled her close. She wriggled free and shook her head. She didn't want to pair up with anyone.

The man reached for her again and she put more space between them. Why couldn't another dancer slip in so she could blend into the rest of the crowd and disappear?

The man's eyes, visible despite the mask, glared at her. He snapped his fingers.

She shook her head again. She wasn't in the BDSM club and wasn't about to submit to someone she didn't know.

The scent of cologne returned and another set of hands touched her waist. A man stepped between her and the interloper. She couldn't see much of this man's face, but he had the body she'd lusted after at Sixxes.

"There you are," he whispered. He glanced back at the other man. The music seemed to soften for a moment. "Sorry," he said. "She's taken."

She glanced over her shoulder. A second man, with a blue mask, stood right behind her.

"Done dancing for now?" Cologne man asked. "We've been dying to join you."

"Is it our turn?" the blue mask man asked.

She switched her gaze between them. "Yes."

Cologne man waved off the interloper. "Have a good night." He turned his attention back to Darinda. "Better?"

She nodded as the music swelled, blotting out any chance of verbally replying. The way the men held her, swayed with her and the tickle of their breath on her skin added to her pleasure. Hell, it all turned her on. She looked at cologne man and her mouth watered. Tall, dark hair, thin, but muscled...she couldn't really see his face, but she didn't need to. His commanding presence attracted her.

A man like him, so overtly sexy, had to be married or in a relationship.

She liked the way she fit between these two men. Like they'd been made for her. Or she'd been made for them. When cologne man brushed his hand across her breast, she arched into him. If he asked her to go to one of the alcoves for sex, she'd accompany him in a heartbeat.

A woman glared at her and she bristled. Who was this person?

The men turned her around so instead of facing the taller of the two, she faced the other. The change in position didn't dampen her excitement. She fit just as well between them this way. She grinded both guys, rubbing her ass against the bulge in the second man's pants and sliding her hands over the first man's chest. The guys smelled wonderful. Like heaven. She wanted to get drunk on this scent. Drunk on this feeling. They were the kind of men that took care of a woman, she could just tell. But she wasn't theirs. She was another club kid dancing. They'd been her knights in shining virgin wool, but nothing more.

When the song ended, the guys led her from the dance floor to the bar.

She wanted to stay with them, but she wasn't in their league. Not a bit. She smiled and touched the first man's cheek, then ran her fingers down the second man's chest before darting away.

She was a street kid who didn't belong anywhere. She lost herself at the clubs. Lost herself in the freedom of the music.

Being with the men made her happy and added to the magic of the evening, but it wasn't meant to last.

She'd have to scurry back to her dingy apartment and the boringness of her life.

She'd had the chance to be someone special, but that wasn't meant to last.

Might as well slice free now and hope the cut hurt less.

It had to, right?

Nick watched her leave, but wanted to grab hold. Good God, she was gorgeous. She felt so wonderful in his arms and didn't seem to be shocked by him or Nathan holding on to her.

She could be the one.

But Suzy was there. She kept gumming up the works. He knew the moment Suzy looked at him. She'd practically shot daggers through Darinda.

He didn't understand why. He and Suzy had split months ago. She hadn't wanted to be shared and wouldn't give Nathan the time of day.

"She left us." Nathan sipped his martini. "I don't like it."

"I don't either, but we can't push her." Nick rested his arm on the bar. "She's coming in Thursday for an interview and I've already earmarked her for employment. I've seen her information and she's a good worker. She'll fit in well."

Nathan crooked his brow. "I've got her earmarked for something else."

"I know you do. I agree one hundred percent, but we have to move slowly. We're trying to go too fast and it'll freak her out." Nick toyed with the condensation on his glass of beer. If he had his way, he'd have Darinda in his bed right now. No question, just her at home with them.

But that was too fast.

"I saw Suzy trying to get in her face." Nathan put the martini down. "I will have her removed."

"Like we had that creep removed that was pushing in on Darinda?" He liked having money and power. Both meant he could get things done. If he wanted something, he had it completed or bought or ordered. "I'll get her out of here."

"I thought you split?"

"We did." He spied Darinda on the dance floor again. Another man had grabbed her, apparently before she'd been able to leave. He wasn't shocked. She was beautiful and men wanted to be with her. He did.

The man grabbed Darinda's breast and Nick saw red. Fuck that bastard. Nick didn't like the way this man kept touching Darinda. Every time she pushed his hands away, the man grabbed at her again.

Nick surged forward and brushed through the crowd to her. When he reached Darinda, he swept her into his arms and tucked her to his chest. He spoke into her ear. "Kiss me."

She brushed her nose along his and nodded, then kissed Nick.

For a split second, nothing else mattered. Just being with her. The dance before had been a teaser for this moment. He cupped the back of her head and opened to her. Darinda grinded on him and sucked on his tongue.

He never wanted to part from her.

When she finally broke the kiss, the man had left and she sighed. Nick kept her close. "Stalker?" he asked. The sparks between him and Darinda were off the charts. Like someone had set off a thousand sticks of dynamite beneath his skin. Like the world widened to him. It changed because of her.

"No." She flattened her palm on his chest. "I always get one or two a night."

He led her back to the edge of the dance floor. He couldn't properly see her face and wished he could. He had the feeling he'd be even more in lust with her. But she couldn't see his face properly, either. He'd managed to do one thing, though. He'd gotten her to open up to him.

"Better?" He offered her a bottle of water. "Are you okay?"

"Thanks." She opened the bottle. "You're not trying to do anything funny? Didn't add something to this?"

"No." Her insinuation annoyed him, even if she had every right to question him. "I don't play that way."

"Then you're one of the few." She downed some of the water. "Nice and cool. Thanks."

"Welcome."

She leaned on the wall. "That guy isn't unusual. Someone always tries to push things that way. They think because I'm here, because the other girls are here and dancing, that we're whores. We're not. There's a woman out there giving me the eye because she thinks I'm trying to take her man. I'm not."

He bit back a laugh. She had no idea how right she was—Suzy hated her because she knew damn well Darinda had taken him. Not that he was Suzy's any longer.

"The guys come here and push in thinking they'll get something that's not for grabs." She shrugged. "I know. I'm wearing this and I'm complaining that I'm not that kind of girl."

"You don't have to explain anything." He debated ripping off his mask. He wanted to tell her exactly who he was, but he didn't. Before he could be sure she was right for his and Nathan's life, he had to see her work.

Not work the club, but at the office. If the money and status didn't drive her, then he'd know she was the one.

He longed to touch her and stroke along her jaw.

"Jesus." Darinda held up the bottle of water. "Thanks for this. Next time, the drink's on me, but I gotta go. She's going to make a scene and I'm not in the mood for it."

"What?" He glanced over his shoulder and spotted Suzy. When he turned back to Darinda, she was gone. God damn it.

Suzy sauntered up to him. She speared her finger in his shoulder and pushed him. "What was that all about? Trying to make me jealous? It's working."

He rolled his eyes and bit back his first response. Arguing with her wasn't going to get him anywhere. "You need to calm down."

"Me?" She folded her arms. "You're trying to make time with a new girl and you want me to calm down."

"What else should I say? I still want to be with you? I don't. You don't want to be with me. You said you wanted me to drop dead." He searched over her shoulder for any sign of Darinda. *No dice. Damn it.*

"I just don't want to be shared." She flipped her hair out of the way. "Do you think she'll let you share her? She'll want to be the only one, just like I do. You should only be with one woman. Me."

He sighed. He'd had enough of this shit. "I'm sorry. I'm not interested. Haven't been since you took my credit card and went shopping. You maxed it out and said I owed you. What do I owe you?"

"A ring." She rested her hand on her hip. "You owe me forever. You promised me I was the only one, then ripped it away."

"You cheated on me." He glared at her. "I'm done. I don't do cheating. You do. Go find the person meant to be with you." He side-stepped her and walked away.

When he crossed the room, he locked gazes with his brother. Nathan looked pissed. Because of Suzy? He rushed over to Nathan. "What's wrong?"

"She's gone."

"I got rid of Suzy, yeah." He followed Nathan to the exit. "Where's Darinda?"

"She's the one who's gone. I paid for her ride home, but she left." Nathan directed him to the car. "I intercepted the driver, so she doesn't have that expense, and I'm sure she's the one we need to hire. She's the one I want in our bed, but I can't push her. You're right—we need to give this time. First, we have to prove to her we're not the same shitty guys like the ones here. She's been hurt a lot and it's up to us to help her heal."

"Agreed." He settled beside his brother in the back of the car. "I get it, though. The sparks when I touched her were off the charts. I've never felt this way before. I want to protect her, kiss her…make love."

"I know." Nathan drummed his fingers on his thigh. "Before we can do any of that, we have to show her we're not out just for sex."

"And know she's not in it for our money."

"Agreed."

"Then it's settled. We want her and she'll be ours." If she wanted to be with them. She could cheat on them like Suzy, but he doubted that. He'd stop at nothing to convince her that he and Nathan would take care of her. They'd found the woman who made them consider changing their lives, but also settling down. She was the one.

She had the ultimate control. If she decided she didn't want to be with them or couldn't handle being with them both, then they'd let her go. They'd bide their time, though, and give her a chance to come to them.

He'd felt the desire swirling through her. When they'd danced, she hadn't pulled away. Instead, she'd touched and delighted in them. She'd made moves, too. She didn't know who they were or their financial status. All she knew was they'd shown interest.

He stared out of the window. Once she worked for them, he and Nathan would put the wheels into motion to bring her to the penthouse.

She wasn't anyone. She was their one and they'd stop at nothing to make the future happen in the way they wanted.

Chapter Three

Darinda sat in the outer office at the Reid firm and waited for the next course of the interview. She'd met with a woman about secretarial work and about filing. She'd shown she could handle the basic filing system. But the woman insisted Darinda had to prove she could use the computer system — which she'd already done a couple of times.

She waited for the next part of the interview. The personal discussion with the head of human resources.

Fine.

She folded her hands on her lap and waited. How long was she supposed to linger? She hadn't been given the chance to leave, yet, and wouldn't risk leaving too soon. She needed the job too much.

An older woman walked into the room. "You're here."

"I am." The gruffness of the woman shocked her. "Should I be gone?"

"I'm surprised you're still here." The woman sat across from her at the desk. "I'll assume you've seen the pay scale, the allocated days off and opportunities for bonuses. You've been reassured you're not getting vacation time for the first six months, yes?"

"I'm aware." She wasn't planning on taking a vacation. Hell, she couldn't afford it.

"You're also aware you'll be in the secretarial pool, yes?"

"I am." If this was a trial by fire, then fine. "Not a problem."

"You're also aware there is no dating among the staff. Meaning, if you decide you want to make a play for the boss, think twice and leave." The woman glared at her again. "We're not a dating service, and the Reid brothers aren't here for your ogling. Understood?"

She nodded once. "I understand."

"They're not dating anyone."

"I wasn't expecting them to date me?" She shook her head. "I just want a job."

"I've had so many women come in here telling me that and then it ends the same way. They think someone is interested in them, they're not and there's drama." The woman tapped the papers together. "You've been approved for employment, but I'm not convinced."

"I see." She wasn't sure if she should be excited or confused. "Thank you?"

"Don't thank me yet." The woman shook her head and left her desk. "You've got to be kidding me. If it's not one thing, it's another. Excuse me."

She left the room and Darinda to her own devices. Darinda debated her next move. She hadn't been given the go ahead to leave, so instead of exiting, she remained in her seat.

The door opened and a man strolled into the room. He smiled and Darinda swore the wattage could light up a small town. His smile also kicked up the heat in her veins. She wasn't sure who this man was, but she'd never had this kind of reaction before. She flattened her hands to hide the trembling. "Hi," she managed. "She just left."

"I know she did." He left a file folder on the desk, then rounded to the front and sat beside her on the sofa. "You're the new hire?"

"I guess I am, I think." She forced a smile, then frowned. "Whoever that lady was, she never said, she's angry. I don't think she likes me. Or she doesn't like that I got the green light."

He laced his fingers together. "She doesn't like anyone. She's been asking for a raise and complaining she's being worked too hard. Everyone has to work hard here. Did she tell you that?"

"She did." She relaxed a bit. At least he was easy to talk to. "She mentioned that, and really made sure I knew I wasn't supposed to date anyone who works here. Interoffice dating is forbidden."

He sighed. "Ah, yes. It is, but she didn't have to be quite so blunt." He smiled again and rested his elbows on his knees. "There has been some issue with people dating before. When they get together, it's fine. Then they break up and they have animosity. One couple had to have legal intervention and we can't do that when they work for us."

"That makes sense, and makes it hard." She fiddled with the clasp on her purse. "She never did tell me when I need to start, or times. Just that I'm hired, I think. It's all rather unclear."

He shifted in his seat and she caught the scent of cologne. She knew that scent. The same one from the club. Was he one of the men she'd danced with? One of her rescuers? Couldn't be. This guy looked like he was just another person in the office. The man from the club reeked of power and money. Not that she cared. Money and power weren't everything. If he was, then she had a problem. She couldn't date the man she'd rubbed all over if they both worked here. Besides, this one was too buttoned-up.

He might be the man from the club and the overall look could've been a front. She had a different overall appearance when she clubbed. She'd never think of revealing her body at work, but the moment she stepped on the dance floor, she wanted to be nearly naked.

Right now, that didn't matter.

"I don't have every bit of information, but I can tell you that you've been hired. You'll start Monday, at nine in the morning. Report at half past eight. You'll get half an hour for lunch and have two fifteen-minute breaks. We do have a code of conduct here, and I'm guessing she didn't give you that. No?"

"No." She'd have paid attention to a code of conduct.

He offered over a folder and her hand brushed his slightly. Sparks shot from her fingertips to her heart, then down to her pussy. *Fuck.* If she had to work next to this guy, she might as well just quit now. She met his gaze for a moment, then averted hers.

"You'll get the information packet via your email as well, but here's the physical copy so you have additional reference. We're glad you're part of the firm and welcome you." He stood when she did and offered his hand. "Welcome to the firm."

She shook hands with him and didn't want to pull away. He smelled good. Like heaven. She accepted the folder. "Thank you. I won't let you down." She paused for a moment. "I'm Darinda Mace, but I didn't catch your name or title." She should probably know both.

"Oh, me." He smiled again and shoved his hands into his pockets. "My name's Alan. I'm an office lackey."

"Well, Alan, office lackey, it's nice to meet you. I hope to see you again." She fidgeted. "I should go. See you on Monday?"

"You will." He waved. "I'm always here."

She nodded and waved, then turned on her heel and left the office. She waited until she stood outside the building to whoop. She'd gotten the job and started in a few days. The packet explained everything… Finally, things were going her way.

She left the firm and headed home to her apartment. Instead of going out tonight, she'd stay in. She needed to conserve her funds and wanted to get her wardrobe in order for the first week.

Darinda waited for the bus. When it stopped, she climbed aboard. Her phone rang, so she checked the screen—it could be the firm wanting to give her information. The ID read *Mom,* and she swiped to ignore the call until she got home. Her mother could wait.

Part of her wanted to call Chloe and share the great news. The rest of her needed to veg out for the afternoon. If she started working on Monday, her lazy days would certainly be reduced. Better take them while she had them.

She hurried to her apartment and kicked out of her high heeled shoes, then left her purse on the table. She placed the folder with her purse and unhooked her bra.

Her phone rang again and she sighed. Might as well answer it now. She checked the screen and her heart sank. Her mother. Fuck.

She couldn't let it go to voicemail again. She'd done that too many times. Sucking in a ragged breath for fortification, she answered. "Hi, Mom."

"It's about time. You never want to talk to me."

She gritted her teeth. Her mother could be cruel. "I haven't had time."

"Are you busy wasting your money in those clubs? You're never going to meet a rich man that way."

"No, I won't." But she could pretend she was anyone other than a poor girl who'd had to run away from home.

"How's the job hunt coming?" her mother asked.

She settled on the sofa. "I found one. I start Monday."

"Good money?"

"I'm not sure. I didn't ask about the salary." To be honest, she knew how much she'd make hourly, but she wasn't sure if the job could translate to becoming salaried down the road. At the moment, she didn't care. She'd get a glass of wine to celebrate the job, watch a corny romance movie and worry about details tomorrow.

"I'd like to think you got a job with decent money because your dad and I could use a few bucks. We put you through school and would like some compensation for our hard work."

She paused. Their hard work? She'd put herself through school. They hadn't given a penny. "Mom, I don't know what the pay package is, but I'll let you know. I don't have any extra to pass your way, though. I'm barely making ends meet."

"You always did lie."

"What?" She should've expected this from her mother. "That's not true."

39

"You've kept all that money to make sure I don't get any of it. You're being intentionally cruel. We brought you into this world."

"You did." She hated that her mother went right to her greatest hits of insults. Her mother wasn't original and never had been. All she wanted to do was hurt. Unfortunately, her mother knew just where to put the verbal knife. "When I get some extra, I'll make sure I pass it along to you."

"You'd better. You spend all your time in those clubs looking like a whore. I raised you better than that."

No, she hadn't, but Darinda wasn't going to complain. It'd fall on deaf ears anyway. "I'm working for a law firm and I'm hoping to get myself back into the black, so when I have some extra, I'll send it along. What's wrong with Dad that you need the cash?"

"Nothing, but you never know. We spent so much on you and it's your turn to pay us back."

She pinched the bridge of her nose. "I'll keep that in mind."

"You'd better,'" her mother snapped. "I don't want to hear from you until you can help support us, you ungrateful brat." She hung up, leaving Darinda in silence.

A tear slipped down Darinda's cheek. She shouldn't have to put up with such abuse, but that was her parents and her biggest reason for pulling herself up. She might not be able to marry a rich man, might never meet one, but that didn't matter. She'd make this life work and she'd do it on her own.

She had no choice.

The Reid brothers might be her ultimate dream, but they were out of reach. That didn't mean she couldn't fantasize.

Dreams were good enough for now.

* * * *

Nathan didn't want to see her go, but he did like watching her leave. Her ass was the stuff of dreams. Just the right amount of wiggle and plenty to grab. He wanted to tangle up with her in the copy room, by the water cooler, in his office across his desk and in their bed. He wanted to taste her all over and not stop until she cried out his name.

"You're staring."

He snorted, then turned. Gert stood behind him with a stack of folders in hand. She adjusted the weight of the items in her grasp and sighed. "You've been staring at the doorway for a solid fifteen minutes."

"Was I?" He folded his arms and sat on the arm of the sofa. "I suppose I was."

"Do you really think she's a good fit?" She put the papers down on the desk. "She's young."

"She is." He tended to take Gert's opinions and consider them heavily. "What do you think?"

Gert narrowed her eyes. "She's young, seems flighty and not like much of a hard worker. She struck me as the type who will stick around for a couple months, then realize she's not going to get anywhere because of the no fraternization rule."

"That's possible." He hadn't considered she'd be a short timer. "What makes you think she will?"

"She looks like she's looking for a husband. A rich client to take care of her — or to take their money." Gert clicked her tongue. "You're not going to find many workers like me who will give their blood, sweat and tears for this firm."

"You do." He tipped his head, considering her words. "You're still here. I thought today was your day off." He and Nick insisted on giving her a four-day work week.

"It was, but you needed someone to be here to interview the new hire. You made it seem like it was the utmost importance for her to be seen."

He had. "I meant, by us."

She gasped and leaned back a fraction of an inch before she caught herself. "To replace someone?"

"No." He appreciated having Gert as their personal secretary. She did her job, didn't complain much and worked well. She kept her mouth shut, too.

Lately, he'd noticed a change in her.

"You don't need another personal secretary. I hate to tell you, but the finances are fine the way they are and we have plenty of staff," she said. "Maybe you could use someone else in filing. Someone you could hire, then let go when things slow down. Not someone you keep around."

"I know what the finances are. We're doing fine." He'd seen the numbers over the weekend and he knew how he and his brother had invested the money. He and Nathan insisted on having more than enough for the rest of their lives, enough to live well without worry and plenty to pass on whenever or if the chance presented itself. He preferred to stay on top of their finances. Yes, he and his brother spent a lot and played hard, but they worked harder to ensure they had the cash to live the life they desired.

"I hope you are." Gert rifled through the pages on her desk. "She strikes me as the one who will show up here trying to get into your pants."

Her words didn't shock him, but her frankness did. He stared at her, measuring his expression and words. "You think so?"

"I do."

He nodded, giving her time and space to speak her mind. He'd learned over the years that the more he listened, the more information he'd be given.

"You get a lot of women in here that just want money. Take Suzy, for example. She doesn't want your money. She wants to be with Nick because she loves him. She just wants to be with him."

He forced himself to remain unaffected, but inwardly, he wanted to scream. From the moment he'd met Suzy, he'd known she wanted money and status. Suzy expected to be pampered, lavished and showered in whatever she wanted. She didn't care who gave her the money or anything else, as long as she got what she desired. Nick was just the latest in her line of acquisitions.

"It's true."

He nodded and once again measured his breaths. "She's original."

"She's got a great sense to her, too. She knows when people are full of garbage and I bet she'd see right through that girl. You can hire her if you want, but I wouldn't," Gert said. "You're going to get taken for a ride."

"With that girl?"

"Yes." Her reply had no hesitation.

"And Nick would be better off with Suzy?" He couldn't wait to hear the answer to this one.

"Yes." Gert leaned her hip on the desk. "Nick needs someone who can love him, can take care of him and doesn't want anything from him. That's Suzy."

"She doesn't like me much." What would she say to that?

"There's always some friction within family situations. You and Nick need to understand that not everyone wants to be as close as you are, and eventually you have to go more separate ways." Gert flexed her fingers and stood tall. "You have to find what you need to make you happy separate of him. If you've got any thoughts on that other woman making you happy, you need to reconsider. Welcome Suzy back into the fold and be a big family. Let her have the babies she wants, and your brother have the woman of his dreams. There's one out there for you, if you'll just spread your net wider and look a while longer."

Interesting hypothesis from someone who didn't know. He usually trusted Gert, but her thoughts weren't on target. Gert tended to be blunt, which he and Nick both appreciated, but something was off with her. She wasn't usually so approving of Suzy. The moment Suzy showed up on the scene, Gert had called her a gold digger and money grubber. Why would she change her opinion now?

At least she hadn't asked for yet another raise. Every time he turned around, he swore she'd asked for another pay increase. Sure, Gert was their most trusted employee, but the amount of money she wanted was excessive.

"I see." He adjusted his hands in his pockets. He'd have to have a discussion with Nick concerning Suzy. He knew damn well Suzy wasn't back on the scene, but if she had something going with Gert, then they all needed to talk.

"You will see. That girl here isn't good news. She's going to end up leaving in six months—if she lasts that long." Gert shook her head. "Suzy will stick around. She's in this for the long haul."

"She may be." But she wasn't sticking around. He wasn't Suzy's biggest fan and didn't like Suzy and Nick getting involved because he and Nick had to share. They didn't each have a woman—they shared. Suzy hadn't wanted that kind of life. Darinda might not, either, but that didn't mean he and Nick couldn't explore and find out.

"I need to finish this filing." Gert picked up the folders. "You've got cases to review this afternoon, and I'll have everything on your tablet by one."

"Thank you," he said. "I appreciate it." But now he had second thoughts about his choices and those of his brother. He prided himself in being smart and savvy, but something felt off. He couldn't put his finger on the problem.

He waited for Gert to leave, then closed himself in his office. He wanted more time with Darinda and replayed their moments together in his mind. the way she felt in his arms, the scent of her, the sparkle in her eyes and the way she hadn't minded being between them. She'd settled right in the middle, like being there was totally normal.

She could be the one.

No, he knew.

They'd found their girl.

Now they just had to bide their time until the pieces fell into place, but he knew they would.

They had to.

He'd accept nothing less.

Chapter Four

Darinda followed Gavin around the store and tried to keep up. He walked faster than her, which wasn't a shock, but some days she wished his attention span wasn't so short. She spotted a blood-red dress and veered off course. The moment she set eyes on the garment, she wanted it. Sheer material, soft and contoured to the body of whomever wore it. She fingered the fabric. "I love a sexy dress."

"Like that?" Gavin stopped beside her. "It'd be dynamic on you. Good for a scene. Just needs a belt or statement piece to go with it." He whipped out his phone and swiped to a photo of a gigantic red drop stone necklace.

"That's cute." She wasn't sure where she'd wear the dress, but she found her size and plucked the garment from the rack.

"You'll be adorable." Gavin nudged her. "I'm looking for a new paddle. I had a friend offer to make one, but I wanted to see what's here first."

"You have a hundred paddles." She knew. He'd used them all on her backside at one time or another.

Darinda followed him again and her thoughts traveled to her first month of work. She hadn't thought she'd like working for the Reid firm until she had been there a few days. Now she didn't want to work anywhere else. The pay was good and she'd been able to bank a few dollars. She hadn't heard from her mother, but she did have money she could send to them when they begged.

For the first time since she'd started working anywhere, she felt appreciated. She was just a cog in the machine, but she was respected. No one gave her shit for her lifestyle, not that she talked about it. She could go in, chat with her cubicle neighbors, and get her job done.

"I'm headed to Sixxes tonight. Are you interested? I could use someone to sit with me." Gavin waved a dong at her. "What about this one?"

She dodged the sex toy and frowned. "Another demonstration night?"

"Always."

She considered the toy in his hand. "That's a great dong. What's the plan?" She wasn't in the mood to have the faux penis used on her. "When are you going?"

"I'm heading there next. I had to wait on you to get off work—and whomever else you're getting off on—so we could hit the store." Gavin crinkled his nose. "Thought we'd go straight there."

"I suppose." She did want to cut loose and have fun. "I don't have an outfit."

"I know."

"So? What's the plan?"

"You, nude." Gavin grinned. "I've got a collar and leash, but with those shoes and nothing else, you'll be dynamite."

She wanted to balk, but she did like being naked. If given the chance, she did want to go to the club and dancing nude would be fun. "Can I dance in one of the cages?"

"Instead of being touched?" He didn't bother to turn around. "I'd hope so. Don't you have a boyfriend?"

"No." She didn't have time. "No one asked me."

"That's a shame."

"You don't want to be with me."

He finally looked at her. "Dar, I'm not settling down."

"Duh." She rolled her eyes. "I don't expect you to, but I meant, you're not asking me and no one else is interested."

He stared at her. "I want you to be able to find someone. You're beautiful, young, smart... You're a catch."

"I'm good enough." She'd been too used to self-depreciation.

"You're more than that," he said. "You're the one I want, but I can't have you because I'm not settling down. I have too much to do and you don't need to wait on me."

"Thanks." She couldn't fault him for being honest.

"I heard a rumor that Nathan and Nick Reid frequent Sixxes. Would you believe it?" Gavin asked. "They met their last girlfriends there."

"Lucky women." She doubted the brothers would be there now. "They're elegant."

"They are, but they have needs, and there's nothing wrong with letting your kinks rule." Gavin produced his phone again. "I know they were there, though, because I saw Nick's girlfriend."

"You did?"

"I did. See?" He held the phone for her and swiped to a photo of a leggy blonde in the shortest skirt possible. "You've even seen her."

She nodded. Boy, had she. "What's her name?" She'd seen the woman and caught her glare.

"Suzy." Gavin swiped to another photo of her. "She's pretty, but that resting bitch face doesn't help her."

"I remember her." She pushed the device away. "She was at the club the last time I went out and if looks could've killed, I'd be dead. She sent more than daggers my way. I don't know if the brothers were there, but if they were, I didn't see them. I just noticed her glaring."

"She's jealous."

"Territorial." She'd met plenty of women like Suzy. Pushy to a fault and jealous, but also with low self-esteem, despite being gorgeous. "She's pretty, though, and she's sure of it. She's got the confidence I'd kill to have."

"You've got confidence," Gavin said and tucked his phone away. "You don't shy away when we play. Don't seem to mind being nearly or totally nude at the clubs. You just go in and have fun."

"We need to pay for this stuff. It's getting late." It wasn't, but she needed to change the subject. She made her way to the register and placed her dress on the counter as she waited for Gavin to pay for the items.

He didn't say anything to her until they were in the car. "You're quiet."

"I am." She folded her arms over her bag. "Sorry."

"No, you're not." He drove them to the club, taking his time along the way. "You've clammed up. What'd I say?"

"The confidence thing. You think I've got it, but I don't. I'm a runaway kid who clubs to lose myself. I don't have self-esteem. I just force myself to do what I do because when I do, I don't have to be me. I'm someone else. Someone who's pretty and fun. Someone who wasn't thrown out by their parents and is barely getting by."

He parked in one of the spots in the garage and switched off the engine, then stared at her. "You've got a lot of things you don't realize."

"I know. I've got good friends, a fantastic job and a place to live. I'm rich in a lot of ways, but I'm terrible with men. I allow myself to get used, I don't stand up enough and I want things I can't have."

"Stop." He placed his hand on hers. "You know you and I aren't dating material for each other, right?"

"I know." She didn't mind that he wasn't boyfriend material. She wasn't sure she wanted to date him anyway.

"There is someone out there for you who isn't going to back down when your parents get pushy, isn't going to be afraid of your kinks and will help you fly. Maybe there's a couple people out there, I don't know. What I do know is that you're gorgeous, you're funny and you're the best thing to happen to me, because you are confident. It takes balls to leave a dangerous, desperate situation and pull yourself up. That's huge."

She shrugged. "Maybe." She wasn't convinced, but what was new? Belief in herself was sometimes hard to come by. "We should go in. What do you want me to do?"

"I'm being watched, but I'm going to be formally offered a position as a club Dom, so what I need from you is to be entourage, really. The leash, collar and heels, stay with me, show you're my sub, but we aren't going to scene. What do you think?"

"Can I dance?"

"Sure can."

She shrugged out of her jacket and blouse "Let's go." If she could dance, forget her problems and have a good time, then she was all in. "I'm ready."

* * * *

Nick followed Nathan into Sixxes and thanked Christ they could go through the celebrity entrance. He hated the term celebrity, but if using that doorway afforded them privacy, then he'd use it. When he and his brother showed up, he wanted to be just another one of the players. Sure, they paid for special privileges, but he liked to blend in.

He had too much on his mind tonight and needed a fun time. Every one of the most recent run-ins with Suzy bothered him. She wanted to be more than exes and wasn't going to stop until they were back together. He didn't want a second round with her. The tumult was too much to handle. The screaming, the spending, the stealing, the demanding. She wanted more, more, more. Money wasn't an issue for him, but her need for that cash, wanting him to spend it all on her, the constant fighting…it was too much.

He donned the mask and joined Nathan in the common room. One of the things he and his brother loved—one of the things that Suzy would never understand—was their desire to share their woman as well as watch. He loved playing the voyeur. She wanted to be on display and draw attention. Not him. Sure, he wore expensive clothes, had fancy watches and drove a high-end vehicle, but he'd rather observe.

Nick sat on the couch with his brother on one of the armchairs. The dancers would be at full throttle and the Doms and subs would be parading soon. There'd be plenty to watch and sate his desires.

He swept his gaze over the dancers and noticed the blond. Darinda. She might have a mask on, but he knew that body. He tapped his brother on the arm.

Nathan said nothing, but nodded as he homed in on Darinda.

Nick's mouth watered. When she moved, she drew him in. She had confidence, style...and that body. He wanted to run his hands all over her again and pull her tight to his chest. Wanted to feel her dance between him and Nathan. Look into her eyes when she blew him, or when they made love. To feel her sweet pussy clench around him. He just knew she'd be made for him.

For them.

Darinda danced and her hair fluttered, then she turned with her body on full display. Her breasts jiggled and nipples beaded. He longed to run his hands over her chest, then spank her sweet little ass.

She seemed to look at him, but probably in his direction. He didn't care. He wasn't ready to make a move on her yet. That didn't mean he couldn't fantasize, watch and drool over her.

She ran her hands down her hips, shimmied, then spun around to give him a view of her ass.

Fuck, yes. He loved that Sixxes offered so much freedom to the players. She could be nude and tantalizing everyone there.

Especially him.

He glanced over at Nathan, who seemed laser focused on her. He nodded to his brother. "Like what you see?"

Nathan dipped his head once. "We can't wait much longer."

"Agreed." They needed to be sure she wasn't already involved with someone before they made a move. He wasn't afraid to take who or what he wanted, but he didn't step in on other people's relationships.

Darinda continued to dance and sway, moving to the music. Like no one, and everyone, watched her. He'd seen her personnel file. She had plenty of cares, but she moved like she had none. Her family intruded on her life, she'd left home at a tender age and put herself through school. She embodied strength and determination, all in a nude dancing package.

She stopped dancing and bowed her head, then walked over to the Dom she'd played with the last time he'd watched her. The Dom clicked a leash onto the D-ring on her collar, then led her across the room to the main playroom. She clasped her hands behind her back and allowed him to walk her to the group of people.

Nick balled his hand. He wasn't in the mood to see her in a scene—not one that he wasn't involved in. Call him a territorial bastard, but he'd set his sights on her and wasn't about to share, except with his brother. If it wasn't poor form and a power play on his part, he'd intervene and take her to his side. He'd make her his sub for the evening, then take her home and never let her go.

Except he'd scare her off that way. She didn't know him as anyone but one of the guys around the office. She'd interacted with Nathan, but it was too soon to claim her. Not that he didn't want to. He knew who he wanted and would stop at nothing to get her.

The Dom stopped at one of the other chairs. He snapped his fingers and she settled on the floor at his feet. He sat down, then rested his hand on the top of her head, petting her hair. She leaned into him, her temple against his thigh as he continued to touch her hair.

The positioning was tender and sweet — if she hadn't been nude and the Dom fully clothed. Nick liked the view, though, and wanted to recreate it at the penthouse.

The germ of an idea formed in his mind. He'd have to confer with Nathan, but he didn't doubt his brother would be on board. He'd make a move on Darinda, invite her to join them for a date, allow her use of the lower floor of the penthouse, then offer her the chance to be their kept woman. Truth be told, he didn't want her that way. He wanted her as their third, but he'd have to bide his time a little longer.

He watched Darinda and, although she seemed submissive, he detected a streak of defiance in her. She angled herself like she was being watched. Was she showing off for them? Offering herself up?

A couple walked onto the platform and the sub knelt before the Dom. Nick watched the scene, but none of it enticed him. He'd rather pay attention to Darinda. She seemed to like being on display, not that he couldn't tell from the way she danced. She liked the attention and being sexy.

God, she drew him in.

When the scene ended, Nick tapped his brother on the arm. Darinda and her Dom were still there, but he wanted to leave. He waited for Nathan, then exited the main playroom.

"What's wrong?" Nathan removed his mask. His ruffled hair was out of place and he smoothed it back into the usual style. "You got out of there quickly. I was enjoying watching Darinda. The more I see her, the more I want her."

"I do, too."

"Then what's the issue?"

"I don't want to see her with him. I want her in our arms." It wasn't the best thing to say because it wasn't possible yet, but that didn't stop him. "She doesn't belong with that Dom."

"He has control over her, but she's not his girl." Nathan opened the door for him, allowing Nick to climb into the backseat first. "She's just there to make him look good."

"How do you know?"

Nathan joined him on the bench seat. "Because she doesn't look at him with longing. With love. He's not looking at her like a lover or protector. He looks at her like she's a piece of meat. He's trying to find another sub. Hell, he's showing off his skills because he was given a job here."

"He's using her?" That pissed him off.

"Not exactly. She's using him, too. She's enjoying time at the club on his dime." Nathan shrugged. "It's not as terrible as it sounds, because she's helping him and he's treating her."

"I don't like it."

"You don't like it because you're an honorable guy and you want her. I don't like it because I don't want everyone watching her that way when we're not in control." Nathan clicked his belt into place. "I don't want to own her, but I don't want to share her, either."

"Then we need to form a plan." Nick watched the scenery out of the window. "We want her and we're just about positive she fits into our lives."

"She does," Nathan said. "So what do we do? Call her into the office? Under what pretense?"

"Something that's plausible." His phone buzzed in his pocket. He withdrew the device and checked it. Gert. "Why are we being called after hours?"

"Gert?"

"Uh-huh." He swiped to retrieve the voicemail. "I don't know what she wants."

"She's been putting in extra hours lately," Nathan said. "And keeps asking for raises. I can't see anything in her files that explains why she needs the money."

"She used to have a gambling problem. Maybe it's back?" He listened to the voicemail.

"Nicholas, I've been at the office. The files are in shape and you're caught up. Your cases for Monday are all in order and attorneys have been assigned for the newest cases. I handled your calls for the day. I've got messages from the bank as well as Suzy. You really should call her back. She's a wonderful woman, and you're not being nice to her. I need to take a break tonight, but I'll be in tomorrow morning to finish getting caught up. Call me if you have questions."

He let the message end, then stared at his brother. "You've got to listen to this." He offered the phone to Nathan.

Nathan hit play and let the voicemail run, then shook his head. "I don't get why she wants you and Suzy together. She didn't even like Suzy when you first brought her around."

"Think they've formed an alliance?" Nick put the phone away. He wasn't calling their personal secretary tonight, or even tomorrow. She might be putting in extra hours, but he wasn't this weekend. He needed time to think about his next steps with Darinda.

"I didn't think they liked each other, but who knows. Suzy is crafty and if she thinks she can get a leg up with Gert, she'll exploit the chance." Nathan scrubbed the back of his hand across his mouth. "Concerning Darinda, we call her into the office. How about a performance review? She won't have to worry that she's in trouble. It's simply a way to check that she's doing what she needs to be doing and we can have her alone."

"I like it." He liked the idea a lot. "And it doesn't look like we're showing favoritism."

"Everyone thinks that," Nathan said. "She got hired on too easily and the word spread that we're looking for a third. I'm sure it's come through the rumor mill."

"Probably." He settled back in his seat and closed his eyes. Now that he and Nathan had a plan to claim Darinda, he could rest. It wouldn't be much longer before she was in his arms and between them. She'd be their girl.

He opened his eyes and sat up as the car stopped. "Nate?"

"Yeah?" Nathan left the vehicle first, then rounded to Nick's side. "What's up?"

"Do you think she's our future?" he asked and exited the car. "We found the one?"

"I can't be completely sure, but it feels right." Nathan waited for him. "We play a little, take her out and see how she reacts. She's special and I can't shake the feeling that she's the one. I'm not rushing it, but I want to."

He nodded. "I want to, too." Nathan was the one who thought things out and took his time. Nick tended to move on instinct. If he and his brother both had the same idea concerning Darinda, then this had to be something special. Had to be fated.

He snorted as he followed his brother up to the penthouse. He didn't believe in fate — not when he had the funds and opportunity to make the future be whatever he desired — but this was different.

He wanted her. Nathan did, too.

She'd be theirs.

No question.

Now to make the dream a reality.

Chapter Five

"My bosses will never look at me like that." Darinda shook her head. She watched superiors, Nick and Nathan Reid, stroll into their office. They couldn't hear her and hadn't noticed her. Hell, they weren't going to, not when she served as a lower-level secretary. They had plenty of other workers at their command.

She barely registered.

Chloe elbowed her. "Maybe not, but you're not full of silicone and can smile."

"I can." She laughed at her friend's comment. Good God. So many of the people she worked with were damn near fake. She wasn't one for bashing other women, but she saw no need to fill her face so much she couldn't move it.

Joy, one of Nick's personal secretaries, hurried after him and nearly tipped over on her high-heeled shoes.

Chloe cocked her brow. "Those heels should be outlawed."

"If they make her feel sexy." Darinda shrugged. "I can't manage them, but she seems to be okay." Okay was an overstatement. Barely keeping upright was more like it.

"You don't wear those?" Chloe snorted and closed her laptop. "I bet you're the type who goes out to the clubs and gets absolutely slutty. I bet you wear latex dresses and thigh high boots. No panties, no bra. Just let it all hang out, and you're probably stunning while you do."

"No." Darinda swore her cheeks burned. How in the hell did Chloe have her number down so well? She'd never told anyone about her habits at the clubs. She dressed up and wore her makeup much darker to hide her identity as much as possible. Sometimes she even wore masks or jewels to disguise her appearance. She had three different latex dresses she loved and a couple fishnet versions that made her feel powerful.

"You're so full of it. Look at you! If you're not going out and having a good time while slaying hearts along the way, I'd be surprised." Chloe flipped her hair over her shoulder. "You've got a killer body, sweet smile and attitude to boot. Guys should be falling at your feet. I bet you'd even be a good dominant."

"Nah." Playing with Gavin didn't count. He served as her Dom when she dabbled, but she wanted something stronger. No, someone stronger.

"You're so coy," Chloe said. "I get it. You're playing with the boys to make them jealous. Get the best offer. Run the table. Smart."

"Something like that." Truth be told, she hadn't found a man who made her motor run that way. She longed to be touched, caressed, embraced. To have someone look her in the eye in such a manner she practically came. A kiss to set her on fire. Hands on her body, electricity in the air.

The guys at the club didn't do that.

Not even close.

Except the two she kept seeing. They were exactly what she wanted — strong, dominant and oozing with power, but they hadn't noticed her. If they had, then they weren't making a move.

"I heard a rumor that the Reid Law Firm is going to add a new partner. Probably Ronna McClark. She's been angling for Nathan for years." Chloe opened the drawer of her desk. "I'm running to the bathroom. Want to join?"

"I'm okay." She stared at the corridor leading to the partners' offices. She'd been with the Reid Firm for a few months and only ventured down that hallway once. She doubted her bosses even knew she was there. But she'd seen the woman Chloe claimed might be the next partner. Ronna was a good lawyer, but she wasn't trying to get into anyone's bed — not anyone male.

She logged out of her screen and closed her laptop, then retrieved her wristlet from the drawer. Once satisfied she had everything, she left her chair.

"Excuse me." Lester Call, the head of security, stopped her. "Ms. Mace?"

"Les." She held on to her bag. "What can I do for you?"

"I need you to come to my office. You're the next one on the list for a performance review."

She stared at the security guard. *Performance review?* She tended to gossip too much with Chloe, but the rest of the office chattered amongst themselves. Otherwise, she kept her head down and did what was asked. Besides, the contract package hadn't mentioned anything about a performance review this fast. After a year, yes but not after three months. "Right now?"

"Yes, please." He slid his hand around her forearm. "It's important. Some of the others have taken too long and we're behind schedule in getting them done."

"Sure." She clutched her bag with one hand and allowed him to tug her across the office. Her coworkers peeked over at her. No one said a word, but she felt them staring at her. She hadn't done anything wrong. If the firm wanted to review her performance, then fine. Let them.

One of the biggest tenets of the Reid Firm was competition. Everyone competed with everyone else to be the best in their job. Secretaries to get more paperwork accomplished, the lawyers to win more cases, the cleaning staff to keep the office immaculate. She and Chloe weren't as interested in the cutthroat aspects, but they liked to challenge each other.

She passed the restroom on the way to her destination. Once Lester closed the door to the security office, she held on to her bag with both hands. "This wasn't mentioned in my contract. Is this something that happens at random?"

"Employees are chosen at random for these reviews just to be sure things are fine. Consider it also a status check. We want to make sure you're happy, have what you need and if there are any problems, they can be addressed early on." Lester nodded to the plastic chair. "Please sit."

"That makes sense, but may I stand? I've been cooped up at my desk all day. I'd like to stretch." Energy surged through her and she needed to move.

"Sure." Lester left the room and the silence enveloped her. She couldn't even hear the music playing over the speaker system. A chill curled around her and reached for her jacket.

When she turned to grab the garment from the chair, the other door opened. She glanced over her shoulder.

Nathan Reid stepped into the room. "Hello. I'm here for your performance review."

She gasped. "You are?"

"You expected someone else would do this?" he asked.

"Sir, I don't mind being reviewed. My performance speaks for itself. I do my job and am competitive. Review me, but why are you doing it? Shouldn't the head of HR be here?"

He cocked his brow, then stared at her. "Head of HR?"

"Isn't that who handles reviews?" She stood firm. "Or is this some kind of farce?"

He didn't speak right away and instead gave her a stony glare in return.

If she'd been in a club, she'd have swept her gaze over him to size up her prey. She'd get what she wanted from him, then leave him begging for more. She'd never considered making a move on Nathan because he was her boss. Offering sex might not get her out of trouble, especially since she still wasn't sure what she'd done. She caught the scent of cologne and realization hit hard. She knew that smell. The rich guy from the clubs who'd danced with her. Who'd watched her. He'd been there.

And now he was her boss.

Fuck.

"Are you considering firing me?" She squared her shoulders. "I have the right to know."

"You do, and I'm not." He remained standing and widened his stance. "You're peculiar."

"I am?" Why would he say that? "How so?"

"You are."

She bit back a growl. "And? As long as I get my job done, being a little odd isn't a bad thing."

"No, it's not."

He made almost no sense. He shouldn't be doing the review, but he also shouldn't be making eyes at her at the club. Something didn't add up. "Look, I know I gossip with Chloe too much, but I haven't colored outside the lines otherwise. I like my job and work hard to do everything else according to the rules. I don't want to lose this gig."

"I never said you were going to."

"Oh." She'd lost her tough facade, but she didn't care. Toughness didn't always matter. "I like working here."

He remained standing, but tipped his head.

"If you're going to ask me what I'm willing to do to keep this job, I'm not foolish. I'm not going to drop to my knees and suck you off right now." She wasn't sure why she'd said that, but sometimes the words tumbled out faster than she could keep them contained. "I'm sorry."

He nodded once. "No need to be sorry."

"I spoke out of turn. That's a big reason to be sorry."

"You don't have to be sorry." He handed her a tablet. "Check your information on this file and I'll be right back."

"Sure." She accepted the device. She'd filled out the information in her onboarding session three months ago. Nothing seemed out of place. In fact, it was exactly the same as she'd given. When she looked up, Nick and

Nathan Reid stared at her and a shiver ran the length of her spine. The predatory nature of their expression both unnerved and enraged her. It also sent electricity through her veins.

Nick sat across from her on the other chair, while Nathan stood in the doorway. Nick laced his fingers together. "Photographs have crossed our desk and we'd like to discuss these images with you. As you know, the firm prides itself on professionalism."

Photos? Where in the hell would they get something like that? The only possibility was they'd been to Sixxes. But where would they have taken them? And when? Going out wasn't being unprofessional. Her off hours were her private time, but she'd been caught clubbing. How could they not catch her? They'd been dancing with her. They'd watched her scene at. Let them question her—she'd be honest, but firm. She didn't have to be tough. Besides, she hadn't done anything wrong. Going out and dressing sexy wasn't a crime.

"I'm sure there are photos. I've been to the clubs and I enjoy it. I was in private spaces and expected privacy, but I never acted with anything but professionalism." She leveled her shoulders, expecting to be fired. Tough shit. Let them. She wasn't ashamed of what she'd done.

"Excuse me. We'll be right back." Nathan left the room first. Nick said nothing as he ducked out of the office.

Yes, the firm didn't have any room for troublemakers. She wasn't a troublemaker, but sometimes that wasn't enough for salvation. She knew that all too well.

A memory hit her and she paused for a second. Salvation. One night as a teenager had changed the entirety of her life. She could still hear her father calling her a whore. The venom in his voice. The fury in his eyes. She hadn't done anything wrong, but she'd been persecuted for her supposed crime.

She'd slept with her boyfriend. She'd embraced her sexuality and reveled in it, starting on her eighteenth birthday. Sexy clothes, harnessing the power of her body, finding comfort in her sensuality…like the pieces of her life made sense. She'd found something within her.

So many other teens had done the same things, but her father had used that indiscretion to kick her out.

Fuck him.

She'd made good with her life. Finished school, put herself through college and now worked for a well-established law firm.

For now.

If her bosses wanted to belittle her like her father, then she'd find a new job—after she stood up for herself. No one had the right to treat her like shit ever again.

Not even the two most important men in the office.

So much for her performance review…

Chapter Six

Nathan Reid paced the length of the inner office he shared with his brother. He and Nick had built the firm over the last twenty years, working to create a law practice that embodied fairness and professionalism. Their staff was expected to behave with the same professionalism.

Except he and his brother weren't always good boys. They'd made plenty of money, obscene amounts really. They could have anything they wanted. Right now, they wanted Darinda. Had since he'd first laid eyes on her.

"What's taking you so long?" Nick snorted. "We left her there, stewing over what she's done, which isn't bad. It's not right. We said it's a performance review, not the firing squad."

His younger brother could be so impatient. Only ten months apart, he and Nick were nearly inseparable. They'd been confused as twins more times than he could count. As close as they were, they might as well have been twins. He wasn't a fan of waiting, either, but this was worth the effort.

Nathan folded his arms. His watch glinted in the harsh lighting. "We know she was at the club. We danced with her. It's not reason for firing and her going out isn't causing problems here at the office."

"No, she's not." Nick sat on his brother's desk. "I wanted to come in here so we could talk. We've been with her. Kissed her. Touched her."

"I know." He remembered every second and replayed them in his mind frequently. "She's the one I want. What do you think? I can't wait any longer."

"I can't either. Do you think she'll agree?"

"I do." He'd been watching her since the moment he'd first seen her at the clubs. She'd captivated him. All long legs and confidence, but covered in long pantsuits and minimal makeup. She always wore her hair up and rarely smiled. He'd read her personnel file, too. Smart, sassy and independent. "She graduated with honors while living in a homeless shelter. She's rare."

"I can't wrap my mind around it, either. She comes in here all bland and quiet, but the moment she's at the club, she's electric. Practically nude, if not totally, submissive, strong and uninhibited."

"She's the stuff of dreams." He'd admired her confidence, and once he learned her journey, he respected the hell out of her. "I want her."

"I want her, too. You think she'll agree to be with us?" Nick touched the top photo. "She might balk."

"She might hesitate, but I doubt it." He had a good feeling about this situation. She could tell them to fuck off. Hell, he expected it. They hadn't told her the truth about being with her at the club. It wasn't a huge secret, but they hadn't been forthcoming and she could be irritated with their omission. Seeing her in action had been the catalyst for hiring her. She was the one they wanted.

He'd imagined planting her between them and grinding on her lithe body again. He wanted to explore her mind, see the world through her eyes and fuck her senseless. If she wore one of those harnesses or that slinky dress she'd donned to the club, or maybe strutted around naked, he'd come in seconds. Just the image of her in those spiked heels and that sheer garment with nothing underneath got him hard.

"We need to speak to her," Nathan said. "We can't leave her over there freaked out."

Nick stood and smoothed his hands over his suit jacket. "We need to apologize and beg forgiveness for being thick."

He nodded once. "And hope she accepts." He cleared his throat and willed his burgeoning erection to stay contained. "I'll get her." He left through the short corridor leading between the rooms to the outer office. Darinda sat on the sofa, face pale and her eyes wide.

"Come," he said. That was the wrong thing to say to control the blood rushing to his dick. "Come along."

Darinda followed him into their inner sanctum. "Sirs. This is the strangest performance review I've ever had."

God, he wanted to hear that coming from her lips for so long. "Ms. Mace."

Nick strode up to her first and offered his hand. "I'm glad you're here."

"Thank you?" She narrowed her eyes. "I get it. You're lawyers, you're rich and I'm just a secretary, but

I'm missing something here. What's going on? Is this really a performance review?"

Nick glanced at Nathan, then stepped back. Nathan nodded once. "We'll explain everything in a moment. Please, have a seat."

"No." She held up both hands. "I want answers. I've done my job, been as professional as I can, and I've never rocked the boat. I checked my logs. I've turned in everything that's passed my desk and in the correct places. If that's what you're looking for concerning a performance review, then I'm fine. Check me, but I'm good. If there's something else, then please tell me."

He bit back a grin. She'd be the death of them, but he loved her sass. She was right, too. "You have given us everything we've asked for."

"Oh good. I wasn't sure what you were expecting — you said this is a performance review." She held tight to her bag. "I'd like an explanation before I quit."

"You won't be quitting." Nathan held up his hand. "This is simply a formality. Yes, there were photos, but we wanted to be sure you're doing your job and you are. As for bringing you in here, we wanted to speak to you. But you're not quitting."

She frowned. "I don't understand."

"We need to tell her," Nick said and picked up one of the folders on his desk. "We've danced with you at the clubs and watched you. We've been close to you."

Her eyes widened as she spied the images. Her lips parted and she squeaked, but otherwise said nothing. Her grasp on her bag loosened. She stood tall, but her hands trembled slightly. "Are you going to fire me?"

"We're not interested in firing you," Nathan said. He gestured to the sofa. "Please, sit."

"You want me to leave quietly." She nodded. "I understand."

"I didn't say that." He slid his hand under her elbow. "Please sit. We'd like to talk to you. Please?" He didn't soften this much with anyone else. Not even his brother.

She sank onto the couch and rested her purse on her lap. "I will go without incident."

"That's not what we'd like." Nathan sat beside her and folded his hands. He had to be delicate, but smart about this. "You go out in public like that a lot. Like the freedom of it? The heat? The music?"

A blush infused her cheeks. "I do."

"Do you?" Nick sat on the arm of the sofa. "Often?"

"Look, if you're going to fire me, then do it. Yes, I go out like that and I like it. That's my time to be myself and free. I don't represent the firm and don't want anyone to know I work here. I just want to have fun." She held tight to her bag strap again. "I don't apologize for having fun or dressing that way, but I'm sorry it's impacted my job."

Nathan bit back a growl. "It hasn't."

"What?" Her eyes widened. "Sir?"

He wanted to hear her say that for him and Nick. "We have a proposition for you."

Nick nodded. "Hear us out."

She switched her gaze between them. "Okay…"

Nathan braced himself. He could do deals with corporations and argue in court with ease, but asking her this would take most of his strength. "You're doing a wonderful job as one of our secretaries. We're happy to have you working for us, but we feel your talents would be better suited in another capacity."

"You do?" She shook her head. "I don't have any other talents. I'm a good typist and can input information."

"You graduated from college with a degree in dance and a second in business," Nathan replied. "We know. We checked."

"We did," Nick added.

"I should've known you would." She didn't release her grasp on the purse. "So?"

"Our firm has been built on our expertise with the law and the appearance of class. When you work with us, you're going to get luxury," Nathan said. "We're also active in the community."

"I know." She shrugged. "I've typed up press releases for you."

"You have." Nathan grinned. He'd forgotten about her extra work. "We've attended many of these events alone."

"You go together." She shifted her gaze again between them. "And with a bevy of beautiful women. I know. I've seen the photos."

"Occasionally." Nick pointed to his watch. "Nate."

He knew. Nathan focused on Darinda. "We don't want the occasional pretty woman. We have a proposition for you. We'd like you to be our girlfriend and accompany us to these events. We have a package for you, involving a penthouse, access to clothes, shoes, jewelry and a chef. You'll be well cared for and want for nothing."

"All so I go with you to a banquet?" She frowned. "That's a bit generous and, besides, why me? I'm nobody."

"Who says that?" Nick asked. He jerked, then withdrew his phone. "Shit. I need to take this. I'll leave you to my brother and will assume you're interested in the offer." He left the room and closed the door behind him.

Nathan resumed focusing on her. "It's quite generous, but there's only one choice."

"Why me?" She relaxed a little, but she didn't appear to be happy.

"We don't make this offer lightly. You're correct—many women would be happy to accompany us to the various clubs and banquets, but we don't want just any woman." He leveled his gaze. "I've been watching you since you began working for us. You're beautiful, sweet, obedient and love to dance. You embody everything we're trying to highlight, as well, but that's not what grabbed my attention."

"Those pictures did."

Among other things. He stared at her chest for a moment. God help him, he wanted to bury his face in her tits. She had great breasts. His mouth watered and he bit back a groan. "They did, but I'm also attracted to you. I'm picky when it comes to women."

"You want beautiful ones."

He'd come to like her smart mouth, too. "You're beautiful, but you're quick on your feet. You're smart and savvy. I'll bet you don't know I danced with you."

She frowned again. "You did? When?"

Then she hadn't noticed him. Good. "At Exposure for mask night. I wore a burgundy suit. We danced to four songs, two fast and two slow. You grinded on me and your tits damn near popped out of that dress. I kept my arm around you. Remember?"

She stared at him, then parted her lips. She blinked. "Crushed burgundy...I asked you to hold me so the creeper who kept grabbing me would stop because he thought you were my boyfriend."

"You did. Whispered in my ear to not let go." He hadn't wanted to. The more she'd grinded her ass into his crotch, the more he'd wanted to take her home that night. Instead, he'd let her leave and ensured from a distance that she'd made it to her apartment unharmed.

She shook her head again. "I'm not good enough for you. Never will be."

"Who said you're not?" He'd checked her background. So it was rough? His wasn't? "Do you know how Nick and I got to this point in our lives?"

"No." Her eyes widened again. "I read the mission statement and the official passages on the website. You worked your way up to owning this firm."

"We did." He nodded slowly. "But that's not the entire truth."

"Wait." She held up her hands. "Why me? This is crazy." She left her seat and held on to her purse.

"We've picked you because you're adorable, but I'm offering this to you because you're about to turn me down. That's how I know you're honorable. You might not think you're good enough, but you are. Any woman who would turn down our offer and make me work for this is the kind of woman we want in our life."

"We?" She didn't move. "What do you mean, 'we'?"

"Nick and I. We're a package deal." He hadn't bothered to mention that yet. "Nick and I want the same woman."

"So I have to choose between you?" She shook her head a third time. "You've got me mistaken for another woman. I don't think this is right for me."

"A closet full of clothes in your own penthouse, a driver, chef, jewelry, shoes and no expenses…you're not right for that?"

"You know I put myself through school by dancing, right? I didn't advertise that, but I worked in Columbus at the strip joint." She fiddled with her purse strap. "I'll go now."

"You'll stay and you'll listen to me." He stood, but didn't raise his voice. "I know you stripped and I know you're scared. I know you're tough and smart and beautiful. I know I'm attracted to you and I'm not about to take no for an answer."

Her eyes widened again. "I thought you said this was a proposition, which means I can turn you down."

He tipped his head once. "I lied."

Chapter Seven

Darinda wobbled. Of course he'd lied. He'd just offered her something so far beyond her means or even her wildest dreams. She couldn't accept any of those amenities he'd offered. Couldn't even think about them. She barely scraped by with her studio apartment and decent, but dinged car.

Now he'd offered her the moon and stars.

She didn't sit, but rather backed up. "I can't."

"You don't have a choice."

"You'll blackmail me." She nodded. "I should've known." Should've expected he'd do this and would eventually fire her.

"Not a chance." His eyes sparkled. "That night I danced with you, I realized what I wanted. Who I wanted. You."

"Me?"

"We want you as our arm candy and kept woman. Our date, pet, sweetheart and bedmate. Our girl." He offered his hand. "Ours."

"Me?" she repeated in a whisper. "I…"

"Don't tell me you'd rather be a secretary for the rest of your time here." Nathan crooked his brow. "You're a smart girl. You know this is an extraordinary offer."

"I do." She sank onto the sofa. "But why me?"

"Why not you?" He glanced over his shoulder as Nick joined them. "Nick?"

His brother stuffed his hands into his pockets. "Still not sure?"

She had to think, but it was nearly impossible with both men staring at her. They were too beautiful for words. Tall, dark, handsome, rich and dangerous. The power radiating from them overwhelmed her. She wasn't sure she should have this chance, but they'd offered it to her.

Nick sat beside her. "Nate? You've got a phone call."

Nathan's glare increased, but he nodded once and left the room.

She hadn't agreed to anything and wasn't sure she liked him going. If she was going to accept, she wanted them both there.

Nick held out his hand. "What's concerning you?"

"Who says I'm concerned?" *What a liar. Good gravy.*

"It's written all over your face, honey." Nick held her hand. He brushed her knuckles with the pad of his thumb. "Most women would jump at this chance. You're not."

"I don't deserve it." She wasn't about to mince words. "Why did you pick me? Because I wore that outfit?"

"That's one reason. Another is your ease in said dress." He inclined his head to meet her gaze. "It took confidence to wear that and go out in public. It's sexy and shows your personality. What's not to like about that?"

"But you said it wasn't professional." He had her so confused.

"We did, but you're not just any employee." His eyes flashed. "Consider this. You could be the woman between us. The one who unites us. Ours. Imagine dressing up for the fancy galas and banquets, having a penthouse and someone to take care of you. Imagine having two men wanting to please you — in our lives, in our bed, in our playroom."

She froze. "Playroom?" He'd piqued her attention. She longed to have someone command her. To have an entire space to play was even better. "How did you know I'd be interested in that?"

"The latex dress, the fetishwear, the boots." Nick's mouth curled in a half-smile. "Nathan and I watched you play at Sixxes. Do you remember being cuffed to the St. Andrew's cross and being spanked? A believe the Dom used a crop and flogger on your pretty ass. Cream soaked your pussy lips and we saw the glitter. When he turned you around, your excitement glistened on your skin and your sweet little nipples tightened. It took everything Nate and I had not to push him out of the way to take over."

She sucked in a ragged breath. She remembered that night well. She'd shown up in a harness dress with her breasts exposed and danced for the first half of the evening. Once the games had begun, she'd stripped down for her friend, Gavin, and submitted. He wasn't her Dom, but he'd wanted to show off his skills and she trusted him. He'd spanked her until she'd came, showed her off and paraded her to the other players. If she'd have known Nick and Nathan were there, she'd have heartily submitted to them. The power coming from them was more than she could handle and she wanted to drown in it.

"I'm guessing you recall that night." Nick's grin widened. "The glazed look in your eyes tells me I'm right."

"You are." She fought to stay under control. "I did participate, and loved it."

"You could have that all night, every night." He resumed caressing her knuckles. "We wouldn't have asked you if we hadn't believed you'd be interested. The fact you've turned my brother down so far tells me you're honest and worthy. Many women would've jumped at the chance and begged for more money. You're not, and that's something we want. You're *who* we want."

She flattened her free hand on her purse. "Do you know what I've done?"

"We do." Nick nodded once. "We've done an extensive background check. Did it when you were hired and again when we decided to offer you this opportunity."

She didn't reply and continued to think about the chance. She could have their hands on her, commanding her, pampering her. She should jump at it.

"What do you think?" Nick snapped his fingers.

As if on command, the door opened and Nathan returned.

"Did you just summon him?" she asked.

"No." Nathan sat on her other side. "I was on my way in. He's simply showing off." He slid his hand along her spine, rubbing her back.

She sighed. Of course they'd show off. They had to demonstrate their power.

"What are you thinking?" Nathan asked. "Talk to us."

She needed to speak. "You need to know who I am. I've lived. I'm not an innocent like some men might want. I've done things."

"Nothing illegal." Nick curled his fingers under her chin. "We know you're scared."

"I'm certainly that, but I'm leery, too. This is too good to be true. Just be your arm candy?" She bit back a whimper as he caressed her jawline. "It seems impossible. You both could have any woman."

"But we see the longing in your eyes, Dar," Nathan said. He stroked her arm, running his fingertips over her bicep. "We crave you as much as you crave us."

She paused. They'd noticed her desire? "What if I want to try this out first? See if we even like it. What if we don't? What if we start this and realize it's a mistake? It could be a disaster. You might see me naked and decide you don't want this."

"I doubt that," Nick said. "We can have a test drive."

A flash of what could be filled her mind. Naked, between them, one behind her and one in front. Hard flesh. Sinful touches. Two cocks just for her. She whimpered at the thought of being with them both. "Yes."

"You'd like to try it?" Nathan tiled her gaze, forcing her to look at him. "Try us?"

"Yes." She nodded. "I would." She'd be offering up her heart and body, but she didn't care. She needed to see this through.

"Very well." Nathan let go and stood. He pulled a keycard from his pocket. "Use this in the elevator. It'll take you to the penthouse. It'll only go to your unit, so you can't get lost. Select something from the closet and wait. We'll join you shortly."

She'd known the building had more floors. It was plain to see from the outside, but she'd assumed the rest of the space belonged to other businesses. "Right now?"

"Yes." Nick stood with his brother. "Unless you've got something you'd like to discuss."

She should. "I do. If we're going to play, which I assume we will be, then we need negotiations. I'm not offering myself up on a silver platter without some boundaries."

Nick grinned. "We hoped you'd say that."

"We did," Nathan added. "Name your conditions."

"Okay." She paused to compose herself. They respected her enough to negotiate. Good. "My safe word is 'ghost'. It's an unusual safe word, but I don't care. I don't do blood or needles. No tattooing. I'll pass out at the sight of blood and I do pain, but not with needles or knives. I'd prefer not to be bruised. No suffocation or breath play, either. I'll wear a gag, blindfold, hook, plug, clips…but I don't like breath play."

Nathan dipped his head once, then glanced at Nick, whose mouth quirked in a smile. "We don't want to bruise our treasure," Nick said. "I'm not wild about needles, either. Nate's got a tattoo, but that's not my style."

"I appreciate that information." She relaxed a bit again. They looked powerful and scary, but they weren't as demanding as she'd expected.

"As for breath play, not my thing," Nathan said. "Your safe word is fine, and we intend to make this scene fun. You'll scream, but we believe you'll want more."

"I have no doubt I will." She toyed with the card. "I like to watch and be watched, but I don't want to be shared outside of this triad. Want to watch porn? I'm in. Sexy clothes? I'm there. Toys? Yes, please. I'd prefer not to be denigrated, but I love to be dominated."

"Then you're certainly our kind of woman." Nathan offered his arm. "May I walk you up to the penthouse?"

"In the elevator?" She suppressed a grin. "I'd love it. Will you be joining us, Nick?"

"I will, but in a few moments." Nick winked. "Someone has to work around here."

Nathan rolled his eyes. "We don't have to work. That's why we have partners and assistants." He patted her hand. "Shall we go?"

"Please." She dipped her head and allowed him to walk her to the elevator within the suite. "I didn't know this was here." She waited at the steel door.

"We don't advertise it." Nathan swiped his card in front of the reader. "Even Gert doesn't know about this elevator."

She stared at him. Gertrude Rainier was their personal secretary and the keeper of the information. No one got back to their offices without her permission. She knew everything. "You're kidding."

"Nope." He gestured to the now opened door. "After you."

She stepped into the car and her breath lodged in her throat. Every wall of the elevator, save for the door, was made of glass. She caught sight of the city skyline around her and the setting sun filtering light through the car. "This is beautiful."

"That's why it's not advertised. Can you imagine showing this off to everyone? It wouldn't be special any longer." Nathan rubbed her shoulders. "When Nick and I commissioned this building, we insisted on the special access to the other floors. There's a staff elevator and two for the public floors, but this one only goes to the penthouses."

"What if someone in the penthouses gets stuck? Like if there's a fire?"

"Other than staff, we're the only ones here."

She watched the skyline spread out before her as the car rose in the building. "The view really is stunning."

He nuzzled her ear. "It is."

She leaned into him and breathed in the scent of his cologne. She'd dreamed about being in his arms so many times, but she'd sworn he'd never see her. That Nick would ever want her. Now, she had the chance to be desired by both men.

The car stopped and her belly lurched. The dim light from the dome in the car illuminated the space as the doors opened.

"Home, my dear." Nathan allowed her first entry into the penthouse. "What do you think?"

She gasped again. She'd never seen so many windows, such a view in one place, or so much chrome. "This is space age."

"Nah." He laughed and stood beside her. "Just modern."

She trailed her fingers along the couch. "This isn't real leather."

"Nope. It's vegan. Everything in here is cruelty free. Nick and I don't want something to die to get something fancy," Nathan said. "Here's the tablet.

Leave a note in the app and whatever you desire will be brought to you."

"I'm a prisoner?" She faced him. "I don't want to be stuck here. I have a cat and a life."

"I know. We'll have the cat brought over. Your car is being moved to the private garage and we know you're not going to be a prisoner. That's not what we envisioned. You've got freedom to leave and shop and do what you'd like." Nathan sat on the arm of the sofa. "You'll have an allowance, as well."

"It's too much." She held up both hands. "I haven't even seen the rest of the place, but I can tell it's... I don't need this. I have a place."

"Ah, but you haven't seen this?" He slipped her hand into his and led her across the penthouse to the bank of windows to the west. "You can see all around the city."

"I know." It was breathtaking. "Mr. Reid." She wasn't sure how to get out of this now.

"Nathan." He curled his fingers under her chin, much as his brother had done. She wanted to melt into his touch. Behind him, a door opened. "That's what I wanted to show you," he said. "Here."

She frowned as he moved out of the way. "What's this?"

"The playroom." He strode ahead of her into the darkened space. "Ready?"

"I suppose I am." She followed him and kept close, afraid of tripping. A moment later, warm yellow light filled the room. Her breath lodged in her throat. The array of paddles, crops and floggers shocked her – in a good way. She noted the various types of cuffs and blindfolds.

He stood behind her again. "This is all for you."

"You bought this for me?" He had to be joking.

"We bought this for the special woman who would join us. When we saw you, held you, felt you, we were certain we'd found the right one," Nathan said. "You."

She flattened her hands on her thighs and heat enveloped her. She groaned. She wanted everything they could give her as long as she got it at their hands. "My God."

"Happy?" He kissed the back of her head.

She slid her hand onto his and sighed. "I know I will be." She'd be satisfied, tired and very happy. "Please, sir, use me."

"We intend to."

Chapter Eight

Nick finished up the last of the paperwork. He didn't mind trading off with Nathan. One day he manned the firm and the next day Nathan did. But right now, he wanted to be upstairs with Nathan and Darinda. He belonged there. Holding her hand, seeing the longing in her eyes were both nearly his undoing.

Gertrude knocked on the door before entering. "Sir."

"Ms. Rainier." He placed the tablet on his desk. "May I help you?"

"I've locked up this floor and have ensured the rest of the firm cannot get back here. Mr. Thompson and Mr. Steiner are working late with their secretaries. You have a meeting tonight with the head of the Johnson firm. The merger?"

"I remember." He'd have to make the playtime short and remind his brother about the cocktail meeting. Darinda would get her first test as their girl. He hoped she'd find something suitable in the closet for the evening.

"The reservation is set and the restaurant is waiting for your arrival. Do you need anything else from me tonight?" She remained in the doorway. "I've completed the paperwork today and filed what needed to be handled. It's almost seven-forty-five. Will you be staying late?"

"I'll handle it. Thank you for your service today." He dipped his head and walked to the doorway. "Thank you."

"You're welcome." She smiled. "Have a good night."

"I will."

She left him alone in the office.

He waited until her footsteps disappeared, then locked the door behind her. If nothing else, he liked having their space private, especially after hours.

Nick turned off the lights and sprinted for the executive elevator. He couldn't get up to the penthouse fast enough. He snorted as the car rose and he watched the skyline extend around him. Wouldn't she laugh when she realized their penthouse was right above hers and connected by a simple staircase. Whenever they wanted her, they'd have her.

If she'd let them. She still hadn't agreed to the deal.

Still, he liked that he and his brother had finally found a woman capable of handling them both at the same time. A growl rose in his throat. He couldn't forget seeing her at the club. Wearing that ruby-beaded mask and pearls. No blouse. No bra. Just the pearls covering her breasts until they weren't covered. Her skirt had covered her, but left nothing to the imagination.

As an outfit, it wasn't modest.

That's what he liked.

She hadn't fit the code of conduct for the workers at the firm, but he didn't want her to be a simple worker any longer. He wanted a lover and partner. Someone to share with Nathan. He couldn't wait to put her in one of those slinky dresses and have her between him and Nathan out on the town.

The doors opened to the penthouse he shared with his brother and the silence deafened him. They needed another person in their space. Needed to make her theirs for good.

He strode across the living room to the staircase leading to her level of the living quarters. Her voice filtered across the expanse and his heart hammered. She knew how to buckle his knees with just a look.

He left the staircase and hurried into the living room. Nathan stood by the windows, staring out at the setting sun.

For a moment, Nick wondered where she'd gone. When he heard her voice, he knew. She'd been positioned between Nathan and the windows.

A vision formed in his mind and he bit back another groan. Her, naked, being shown off to the world and on her knees. Her ass open to him and her mouth on Nathan's dick. She'd be electric. Gorgeous.

Nathan glanced over his shoulder. "Nick."

He nodded once. "Brother."

Darinda ducked away from Nathan. "Sir."

He'd like to hear that a few more times for the rest of his life. "Darinda."

Nathan straightened and stuffed his hands into his pockets. "Everything under control?"

He snorted. Not for his brother, but that wasn't up for discussion. "It is. I've talked to Gert and our tickets are ready."

"Tickets? Where are you going?" Darinda perched on the arm of the sofa. "I hope you'll tell me about it when you come back."

"Won't have to." Nathan rounded the table and removed his cufflinks. He left them on the granite and loosened his shirt cuffs. "You'll be coming along."

"I will?" she squeaked.

Ah, so innocent, despite her naughty side. "Bad girl, you're our date." Nick withdrew his phone and summoned the stylist. It wouldn't take long to get Darinda ready, but he wanted her to look her best. "The bath is being drawn right now."

"I…" She froze. "Me?"

"That's the idea." Nick met Nathan's gaze. "Unless I'm wrong?"

"Nope." Nathan bobbed his eyebrows, then hooked his fingers in his pockets. "I'll be back in a few. Girl, I expect you to comply. That's part of the deal."

"Yes, sir." She didn't leave her seat.

Nick waited until Nathan left the room, no doubt just on the bottom step and listening to everything. Good, he wanted Nathan to eavesdrop.

Nick stared at her. "Come here."

Without a word, she complied and crossed the room. "Sir."

He enveloped her in his arms. God, she felt good there. He nuzzled her cheek. "What's holding you back?"

"From giving in?"

"Yes." He brushed his thumb across her bottom lip. "Tell me."

"I've done things and you both want someone who has a certain image. I don't have that image."

"Who says you need it?" He guided her to the sofa and sat first, then tugged her onto his lap. "You made an impression on us. I believe it was the pearls."

She blushed from her hairline to her chest. "You saw me?"

"We danced with you." He rubbed her sides along her ribs. "You weren't wearing anything but those pearls and that thin skirt. I could just about see the cream on your pussy."

She shivered and draped her arms around his neck. "You and Nathan were there."

"Positioned around you." He'd been in front that night. "Those ridiculous masks hide so much."

"Not the way you smell." She massaged his shoulders. "I thought I recognized it, but I didn't trust myself."

"You can with us." He pulled her closer. "We'll make sure you're cherished. There's a great big tub in there filling right now for you. A whole closet of clothes at your discretion and a stylist on the way to ensure you're happy."

"So later I can make sure you're happy."

"Not just me. Nathan and I are a packaged deal—like we said." He palmed her ass. "So spankable, naughty girl."

"And you know what all I like?"

"We do." He swatted her butt. "You want to be between us. On your knees. Wearing something from the clubs. Touched. Caressed." He'd almost said loved, but hesitated. He needed to be with her first before he decided if this was really love. He wasn't against love, or falling so fast, but he liked to test drive before he bought. *At least get a good feel for the interior.*

She moaned. "Yes."

He slid his palm across the back of her neck and forced her closer. "Kiss me."

She didn't argue. Instead, she gave in and tilted her head. The kiss sizzled him from his head to his feet and sent blood rushing to his cock. He needed her mouth around his dick right now. He sucked on her tongue and swallowed her whimpers. The way she undulated on him, riding the bulge in his trousers, wasn't practiced. This was sheer reaction.

He held her tight and dug his fingers into her hip. Waiting until later would kill him. He broke the kiss. "Get naked."

She blushed again, then scrambled off his lap. Within seconds, she fumbled out of her dress and suit jacket. The simple cotton panties clung to her hips and the bland bra did little to hide her assets. But paired with the high heeled pumps, she was a knockout. He reached for her before she removed the lingerie or her shoes.

"Want me that much?" She shoved the panties down her legs, baring her lower body.

There was the boldness he'd fallen for. When he pulled her onto his lap, she unhooked her bra. The garment fell to the floor. Her breasts jiggled slightly. Her nipples beaded.

"Damn." Nick tweaked her nipple. "You're stunning."

She gasped. "Thank you."

"I want you on my cock." He unzipped his trousers.

Darinda licked her lips, then helped free him from his silk boxers. Her eyes lit up. "You're… Wow."

He'd been told he had enough to please plenty of times, but he liked her eagerness. "Oh?"

She slid to her knees between his thighs. With her fingers curled around his shaft, she traced the line of her lips with the pre-cum shimmering on the tip of his erection.

The move sent a fresh wave of sizzles through him. He threaded his fingers into her hair. "Do it." He nudged her, guiding her. "I want you on me."

She met his gaze as she swallowed him to the back of her throat. Her hair tickled his hand. The velvet of her tongue, the heat enveloping him and the passion in her eyes nearly undid him. He groaned and slid down in his seat.

"Yes, babe." He rocked into her, pushing his dick deep in her mouth. "More."

She didn't relent and instead increased her speed. She bobbed her head, curling her tongue around him. Her whimpers pushed him right to the edge.

"Fuck," he murmured. He tensed all over. "More."

She flattened her free hand on his thigh and continued to stroke while she bobbed her head.

Nathan entered the room again, but this time, he'd unzipped his trousers. He stood behind her and lifted her hips.

She didn't stop bobbing as Nathan positioned her. He held on to her hips and entered her as she swallowed Nick deep. Within seconds, he'd helped the threesome become one perfect rhythm. Her moans vibrated along Nick's shaft and she let go long enough to dig her hands into his thighs.

Nick petted her hair. "Good girl. Good naughty girl. Fuck. Taking me deep. Come for us. You love his cock in your pussy. I bet you're wet and needy. You want both cocks. Want to come and let go. Do it. We've got you."

She shivered and flexed her fingers. She cried out around his shaft and the sound pushed him over the edge. He jammed his cock between her lips. As he came, he moaned.

"Fuck," Nick growled. He wished he'd used more finesse, but how could he? She felt way too good around him.

Nathan increased the speed of his thrusts. "Fuck, that's hot." He tipped his head back. The sound of him swatting her ass echoed in the penthouse.

Nick slumped in his seat and watched the show. He loved seeing his brother with their woman and it'd been too long since they'd had someone worthy enough to share.

Darinda braced herself on her hands and met his gaze. "Nick."

"Right here." He leaned forward to cup her jaw in his hands. "So beautiful."

"Need to come." The pleading in her eyes cut straight through to his core.

"Come for us. Do it." He caressed her cheeks. "Come apart."

Nathan growled and his moves turned feral. "Coming." He reached around her and slid one hand between her legs.

Her eyes widened and she whimpered. "I can't…"

"You can." Nick slipped his thumb between her lips. "Come for us."

She shivered as Nathan slammed into her. Nathan raked his nails down her hips, then stilled. "Jesus Christ," he managed. He bowed his head. "Blew my mind."

She'd done that for Nick, too. Nick brushed her hair from her face. If this was what she'd do on a whim, he could only imagine what would happen after a night out.

Nathan withdrew, then let go of her. "Bath's ready." He panted and scrubbed one hand across his face. "Go ahead. I'll guide you." He slid his arm around her waist and led her to the bathroom. A moment later, Nathan reappeared and zipped his trousers.

"That was... Wow." Nick pushed his cock back behind his fly, but didn't zip. "I don't want to let this one go."

"I don't, either." Nathan glanced over at the bathroom door. "She's skittish."

"For being so free at the club, you're right." He stood, then folded his arms. "Gert got everything set for tonight. We simply show up, but we've got seats at the table. The clients will want our attention. They're paying well." He'd helped to set up the meeting. The Severin family needed representation and they'd get it. Just not Nick or Nathan at the helm.

"Good." Nathan faced his brother. "I want to take her out tonight, but not just to the restaurant. Something fun, too. Something she'll like."

"Agreed." He liked how he and Nathan tended to be on the same wavelength. "The wharf is open tonight. Think she'd like that?"

"I know she would." Nathan winked. "Let's get ready. It'll take her a little while and she'll want a bit of a rest."

"She will." Nathan followed Nick up the stairs to the penthouse. "We haven't told her this leads to our living space."

"No." He'd figured they would later. "She's got enough to handle right now." He pushed the glass door aside. When he and his brother had created the penthouse suites, they'd assumed they'd be living one above and the other below. The more they'd spent time at the office and discussed their needs with partners, the more they'd realized they wanted to share the same woman. Some women had been good partners, but nothing long-term. Some only wanted him or just Nathan. That wouldn't fly.

"I heard from Suzy today." Nathan stopped at the table. "She's interested in coming back."

"Suzy?" He hadn't thought about her in ages. His brother had been involved with her, but she hadn't wanted anything to do with Nick. The moment they'd realized she wanted to play them off each other, they stopped. She hadn't been interested in being with both of them, but honestly, Nick hadn't trusted her. He didn't like being lied to and she did frequently.

"She called me."

He stared at his brother. "You said you'd blocked her."

"I did, but she conned one of the secretaries to connect my personal number to her. Not a direct dial. Channels." Nathan stripped out of his shirt, then undershirt. He removed his watch. "I've sent down a rule that our numbers are to be given out under no circumstances. There will be no further connections to us, either. Anyone can talk to one of the junior partners. Unless someone has our personal numbers, they can't get access."

"Good." Nick paused. "What did she want? To come back? As...?"

"Our girl." Nathan dropped his pants and tossed the garment into the hamper. "Someone told her we were looking for a new partner. A girl to share."

"And she wants in." He rolled his eyes. "Jesus."

"That's it." Nathan sat on Nick's bed as he removed his socks. "She heard from someone here at the firm that we were looking for someone new. I don't know who let it slip."

"I don't either." He and Nathan kept the search close to his chest. "You don't think she told?"

"Darinda? No." Nathan shook his head. "Her phone records don't show she's had any contact with Suzy. The only conversations she's had are with Chloe, her desk mate. Most of those conversations have been recorded and screened. Our girl has had a thing for us for a while."

"Oh?" He liked hearing that.

"I don't know who Suzy befriended, but I won't rest until I find out and fire them." Nathan balled his socks. "Pisses me off."

"Me as well. I don't like being double crossed. We need security and professionalism here and that's not either." He unbuttoned his shirt. "Nate, being with her was better than I expected. Darinda might be the one."

"You've figured that out after one encounter?" Nathan stood. "I mean, I'm not averse to keeping her."

"Averse?" He snorted. "Nate."

"Yeah, yeah. I want her, too. Want to keep her."

She was the first woman to be invited back to the penthouse and installed there. The first one they'd wanted to spoil rotten. He couldn't see his life without her. "So what do you want to do about it? I'm not about to let her go."

"We give her a few nights she can't forget and sweeten the offer she can't refuse so much that she gives in." Nathan winked. "We get what we want."

He laughed, knowing his brother was right. "We do."

Chapter Nine

Darinda sat in the tub and stared at the tilework. How in the hell had she gotten here? A kid whose parents hadn't wanted her, who'd run wild for ages and didn't deserve to be in the company of two millionaires, was in the tub of a penthouse suite.

The attendant brought in a set of fluffy white towels. She smiled. "May I bring you anything else? The stylist has arrived. If you have no other need for me, then I'll be in the bedroom waiting to dress you."

"I can dress myself." She sat up, staying within the bubbles to hide her boobs, but enough to gain the attendant's attention. "Wait."

"Yes, ma'am." The woman continued to smile, seemingly unbothered by the situation. "What can I get you?"

"Have you worked for them long?" She folded her arms on the edge of the clawfoot tub and rested her chin on her hands. "Is this all you do?"

"I'm their housekeeper, yes." She laced her fingers together. "I've known the boys for twenty years and they take care of me. I might be the housekeeper, but they treat me well and I'm paid handsomely. My family lives with me two floors down, and this job has paid for my kids to go to college. I can't complain."

She hadn't expected the woman to say that. "May I use your name? I feel weird not using it."

"They don't usually invite anyone up here. I've never seen them bring a woman home," the woman said. "My name is Loretta. You can relax. I'm here to take care of you and ensure the boys are happy. I'll ensure you're dressed for dinner tonight."

She frowned as she realized what Loretta had said. "First, thank you. I hope we can be friends," she said. "But wait. They don't bring other women up here?" She wasn't going to have to battle anyone else?

"Nope."

Darinda sloshed in the water, then washed herself before reaching for the plug—except there wasn't one. "How do I drain this?"

"Here." Loretta tapped the side of the tub.

"Is it touch?" She peered over the edge. "Really?"

"Hidden control panel." Loretta laughed and offered over a towel. "The stylist will handle your hair and makeup next while I have the dresses pulled for you."

"Thanks." She stood and wrapped up in the towel. The fabric smelled like lavender and relaxed her. "Holy cow…" Now she had to focus, instead of getting sleepy. "I thought they had all kinds of women."

"I don't like to gossip about the boys, but since you're here, they've deemed you to be special and I'll tell you." Loretta helped her from the tub. "I worked for their parents before I came here. They're good men and devoted to their partners. They've dated a lot, sure, but what men haven't? Nick and Nate might have gone out a lot, but they haven't really settled down. They keep their dates at arms' length."

"But I'm here."

"You are." Loretta rinsed down the tub. "Consider yourself lucky and ride the wave. If you really like them, then be yourself and let them baby you. You must be special or you wouldn't be here, so enjoy it. You seem sweet and just what they want, but don't be surprised by the toy room."

"They showed me." She held tight to the towel. "I'm not surprised."

"Good. Enjoy that, too."

"You're not bothered by it?" she asked. "Holy shit. You have a whole room of dildoes and paddles?"

"I don't use them, but I don't condemn anyone else who does. There's something fun about toys." Loretta stepped aside. "Time to get your hair and makeup done. Go."

"Right." She paused. "I bet they treat you like a queen at Christmas."

"They do, and they will for you as well." Loretta waved her off. "Dinner is also a meeting with clients, so keep that in mind. They're inviting you fully into their world. Take the chance and enjoy it."

"I will." She squared her shoulders and met the stylist in the adjacent room. Time to get glammed up. She had to shine for this dinner tonight.

Absolutely fucking shine.

* * * *

Darinda smoothed the cocktail dress and teetered in her shoes. She'd caught sight of herself in the mirror twice and nearly passed out. She had no lack of confidence in most situations, but between the dress, the hair and makeup, she'd become something out of a fantasy. The lacy panties sent shivers along her spine with every step and the bracelets jingled as she moved. She wasn't this girl. She was simple, but liked to show off. She was sweet, but hardened. She wasn't the kind of woman who should be on their arms. She wasn't date material.

God. Why did this feel so…foreign? Because she'd shown herself off to others, but no one this important or fantastic.

She picked up her phone and tapped the icon for the internet. Once she had the app open, she searched Nick and Nathan. She'd been working for them for three months, but never actually researched them. Part of her worried what she'd find. It wasn't every day that two men had one woman for their date.

The link to the firm came up first, but she switched to the articles. Nick and Nathan could put whatever they wanted on a website. The stories about them by others would tell more of the tale. She tapped the first result — a story about Nick and a woman she'd seen before. Suzy. She gasped. No fucking way. The woman giving her shit was indeed Nick's… She read the story again. Suzy was his ex. She massaged her forehead. Suzy was much prettier. She ran with a higher-class crowd, too.

But they'd broken up. Surely, there had to be a reason. She shook her head. Something didn't add up.

She switched to the photos and searched for a reason why Nick and Nathan needed only one woman. It seemed so odd. They claimed they shared, but come on. Shouldn't they each have someone?

Why was she worrying? This was probably just a business dinner and the other woman would show up. That had to be it. Her upset was for nothing. She swiped to close the tab, then cleared the search from her phone. She'd gotten worked up without reason. Things would be fine.

"Naughty girl?" Nathan entered the suite. "Darinda?"

"Here." She swore her voice evaporated. She cleared her throat and summoned every last ounce of her confidence. "Here."

He caught sight of her and his eyes glittered. "My God."

"Too much?" So much for her confidence. "I get it. This was selected for me, but it's a business dinner. You don't want me this…like this. I'll change." She wasn't sure what she'd change into yet, but she'd figure out something.

"No." He crossed the room and held his hand out to her. "You're a vision. Almost too beautiful to take out tonight. Hell, we should stay in. Fuck the client."

"You can't do that. It's unethical." She allowed him to give her a twirl, then sagged in his embrace. "But if you're meeting with a client, then I'm overdressed. I'll change."

"You'll do no such thing. Dinner tonight is at a fancy restaurant and we're expected to dress accordingly. That dress is more than according. It's perfect, and I will have to up my game in order to be seen beside you." He kissed her. "I'd rather fuck you again — all night long."

She clutched his suit jacket and pressed her thighs together. He sent heat throughout her body. She leaned into the kiss. When she opened to him, he took control and tangled his tongue with hers. He smelled like sin and tasted like champagne.

He'd become her drug. So had Nick. Christ. She'd only been with them once and hadn't even fucked Nick, but she didn't want to go. The perks weren't the draw. Nick and Nathan were. She couldn't wait to experience the playroom with them. But Nick's ex kept hanging around, like she didn't want to be an ex. Maybe the ex and Nick were supposed to be together? Supposed to patch things up? Sure looked that way, and that her threesome with them wasn't going to last.

Those kinds of things never did.

"Hold up. I want in." Nick eased up behind her and slid his hands along her hips. "Feels good, naughty girl."

She liked the name they'd given her. She turned in Nathan's embrace to give Nick attention without leaving Nathan. As she turned, she rubbed her ass against Nathan's crotch. The bulge in his pants pleased her. She kissed Nick and delighted in him clutching her breast. The pain added to her need.

"What about your date?" she asked. "Are we picking up someone else?" She liked the way they held her, but the dream and play would only last so long. Tonight, reality would come through and she'd have to accept she was just a toy.

"We should go." Nick swatted her ass. "Bad girl. You want us to lose this client."

"Maybe." She liked the way they made her feel. She paused. "No, I don't. If we need to pick someone else up, then I'm fine with that. I don't mind."

"Who said that?" Nathan toyed with a lock of her hair. "There isn't anyone else."

"Nope," Nick added. "Just you."

"Me with the both of you?" That seemed so strange and nearly impossible. They had to want someone else involved.

"There is no one else." Nathan let go of her. "Is the car waiting?"

"It is." Nick offered his arm.

"Thank you." She allowed Nick to walk her out of the room and into the elevator. When she glanced backward, she noticed Nathan switching off lights. He quickly joined on the other side, boxing her in when they reached the elevator. "Where are we going?"

She didn't understand. They were so nonchalant about everything. Nothing ever fazed them. She should've done more research and read up on them. Was this the norm for them? Couldn't be.

"We'll meet them at Cider Lake," Nathan replied. He caressed her backside through the silk of her dress.

She groaned as the elevator descended to the ground floor. He and Nick made thinking straight nearly impossible. She pressed her knees together to keep the heat and desire at bay. They had her on the edge and excited. One command and she'd gladly strip for them and be at their discretion.

Wasn't she already at their call? Essentially she was. Was she a kept woman now? Did that entirely bother her? No. It didn't.

Her nerve endings sizzled. She needed to be with them both again. Naked, vulnerable and on her knees.

Still, she wondered if she deserved to be in this situation. Everything felt so impossible, but she refused to apologize for loving where she was — between them.

For the first time in a long while, she felt loved and cherished. Pampered.

Until tonight, she hadn't thought those feelings were possible.

What would happen when they found out the truth about her? Would they toss her aside? Just use her? Tell her to get lost? Any of those possibilities could happen. She pushed her negativity aside. If nothing else, she'd enjoy tonight while she had it and keep good memories for later.

A moment later, the doors opened. Nathan led the way, escorting her to the car.

The black sedan glinted in the light and practically disappeared against the dark sky. The door opened and she spied the interior. Nathan stepped out of the way as Nick entered the vehicle first. She scooted in beside him, then grasped his thigh for stability. She yanked her hand back.

"Sorry." She swore her ears burned.

"Why?"

"I shouldn't be touching you. I'm supposed to be acting dignified, right?" Like in the movies. At least a little better than feeling up her employer.

Nick placed her hand back on his thigh. "I appreciate your caress. Touch me whenever you want."

He did? He'd let her? She bit back a grin as Nathan joined them in the car. Nick slid his arm around her and Nathan patted her thigh where the skirt revealed her skin.

She wasn't sure if the car moved. If it was, she couldn't feel it. All she saw were Nick and Nathan. They consumed her thoughts. Nick tipped her chin, forcing her to look at him. Nothing else mattered for now. She didn't care if there were others joining them or what Nick and Nathan had planned. She simply wanted to be with them.

"Our dirty girl." He kissed her and she swore he drew the breath from her. He palmed her chest with his free hand, squeezing and pinching her breast.

She groaned into the kiss. Her skin tingled.

At the same time, Nathan parted her legs. He slipped his hand between her thighs and pushed the skirt up. The cool air slid over her pussy. No amount of lace would cover her or hide her wetness. She sucked on Nick's tongue and inched closer to him while Nathan caressed her cunt through the thin lace of her panties. She swore she floated.

She shivered.

Nathan grunted. "Fuck."

She opened her eyes, shocked she'd even closed them. What was wrong? She smoothed her skirt down, but stayed close to Nick.

Nick broke the kiss. "What's wrong?"

"We're here already." Nathan helped ease her dress the rest of the way down. "That drive wasn't nearly long enough."

"No, it wasn't." Nick brushed his forehead against hers, then shifted in his seat. "It won't be long until we're home."

She agreed, but opted to put her guard in place. Her heart was at risk, but she trusted them—not that she had much choice. She'd gone along for the ride and had to see it through. She followed Nathan out of the car. The lights on the building were muted, giving an air of sophistication. She'd be willing to bet while the exterior illumination wasn't bright, there had to be tons of cameras watching the place.

Darinda slid her arm around Nathan's, then her other one around Nick's. Her shoes clicked on the bricks as she walked inside. Palms hulked in the corners of the foyer and blood-red paint covered the walls. The plush carpeting covered her footfalls. She didn't see any of the tables.

"Where…" She pressed her lips together to keep the question quiet.

Nathan rubbed her back. "Here." He led her to a table, covered in a cream-colored cloth and decorated with flowers and candles.

The whole scene was romantic. Like a dream. Too good to be true—until she saw the others.

Four men and a woman sat waiting on them and a pang of insecurity hit. "Nathan." She turned her head to keep from being so loud. She didn't belong here. She was a club kid and a secretary. She wasn't a fancy lady. "You can take me home. I don't belong here." She tugged against him, ready to run the hell out of there.

"Relax," he murmured against her temple. He patted her ass, then rubbed her back. "We've got you. You're safe and you belong here. I wouldn't let anyone hurt you or do something to upset you. Promise."

"I trust you," she replied, despite not totally believing him. Fear still gripped her. What if the dinner companions recognized her, or saw her shortcomings? That'd look bad for Nick and Nathan. They could buy anyone. Hell, they should. With their obscene amount of money, they could have a true lady. Not her. There had to be someone else they could be accompanying. "Maybe I should go."

"I'd prefer you stay. I want you here, and so does Nathan," Nick said. "And you're more than just a pretty face. You're our girl."

Although the fear didn't subside, she did her best to relax. She didn't recognize anyone at the table, but then again, she didn't know the people Nick or Nathan ran with. The names were just words on a page to her.

"Not alone?" The bald man stood. "The famous Reid brothers have a girlfriend? I never thought I'd see the day." He laughed and the sound boomed.

Embarrassment swept over her. *Their girlfriend...*

"It takes a special woman to tame us," Nick said. "She did with ease."

Wait. The men were talking about her like she wasn't even there. She shifted her gaze between Nick and Nathan, then the bald man. She'd expected to be going to dinner, not volunteering to be a girlfriend. Not that being their girl would be bad.

"So much that you've mellowed?" the woman asked. "Seems impossible."

Everything seemed impossible. Darinda fought the urge to squirm as she settled in her chair. She hadn't tamed anyone. This was a dinner date and the possibility of being kept. She wasn't a girlfriend. Just a woman at a fancy restaurant.

"Lola. Don't ask questions you already know the answers to," Nathan said. "No one mellows us."

She didn't know how to mellow anyone. She wasn't even sure which fork was the dinner one and which one should be used for salad. *Oh God.* She'd make a fool of herself.

"Maybe I do," Lola said and grinned. "I hope she has. You're easier to work with that way."

"We've never slowed down," Nick said. He gestured to the server as the man poured wine. "Thank you. Now, about why we're here."

Darinda had wondered when they'd get to that. She spied the label on the wine and shock filled her brain. The bottle was so expensive it didn't even have a name, just a design? *Holy shit*. She really didn't deserve to be here. Her wine, when she had any, came from a box.

"After food," the bald man said. "You need to introduce us."

Nathan sighed just loud enough for her to hear it. "Greene Wilton, Lola Nadine, Cory Tupps and Martin Wilson. This is our partner, Darinda Race. Now, the deal."

Partner? She had to have heard him wrong. Her stomach growled and she wanted to hide. Why did the noise have to be audible? She swore the tips of her ears burned. A dignified lady wouldn't be so unnerved.

"We should eat," Greene said. "I'm starving, too."

She wanted to melt into the floor. If he'd heard the sound, then it was too loud. "It is getting close to that time." Did that sound like a good way to cover for her faux pas?

Nathan palmed her thigh. "I'm hungry, too."

She relaxed a bit as he spoke. She'd thought the tryst at the apartment would've been enough to satisfy him. Must be insatiable. "Thanks," she murmured.

Nick palmed her other thigh, parting her legs. Her skirt rode up again and she sucked in a ragged breath. He moved the scrap of lace aside, exposing her pussy under the table. Good thing no one could see. She shivered with anticipation and desire.

Nathan slid his hand up and eased one finger along her slit. Fingering her without penetrating turned her on. A lady might not let them do this to her, but she wanted every last tingle and tantalizing bit of their attention.

"So, the deal." Lola's firm tone grabbed her attention. "We need your representation."

The server placed a salad in front of every diner and Darinda bit back a moan of appreciation. She needed food in her stomach and Nick's fingers in her pussy. God, she was so greedy.

Nathan nudged the correct fork, then folded his hands. "About?"

"We'd like to keep you on retainer for when the deals go south. We need someone who can handle the logistics and legal issues." Cory Tupps stabbed his salad. "What do you think?"

"Unless you'd like to offer over your girl, there." Greene laughed. "She's a beaut."

She fought not to glare at the man. Offer her up? Oh, hell no. She wasn't a commodity and how dare he think she was?

"Offer over?" Nick yanked his hand away and sat up straighter. "I'm sorry?"

That's all he had to say? *I'm sorry?* She wanted to jab Nick in the ribs.

"She's not up for grabs," Nathan said. "And seeing as you're trying to hire us, why would we be interested in giving up something for your business?"

She'd like to know that, too. Jesus Christ. What kind of people wanted to trade human beings for work? She wasn't interested.

"Trying to keep the client happy. She's quite the looker." Greene narrowed his eyes. "Maybe consider sharing."

Her blood chilled and she dropped her fork, the sound clanking loudly. The flames on the candles danced. Greene had to be kidding. Taking her?

Wanting her? He wasn't kidding. Nathan and Nick had better not be serious about sharing her this way.

"I'm sorry." Nathan held up both hands. "You're mistaken."

"I mean, she's beautiful and apparently she's willing." Cory crossed his arms. "We'd like her as collateral. Her naked in the office, at our discretion. Might be good for morale."

She froze. Her worst fears were coming to fruition. She didn't mind being used that way with Nick and Nathan. Truth be told, she deserved to be used and not cherished. But she sure hoped they'd argue to keep her—not hand her over to people she didn't know for reasons she didn't like.

"That's it." Nick stood. "We were here to offer legal advice and talk about the retainer, not human trafficking. This is not going to happen."

"You don't want to share your girl? You share her between each other." Lola shrugged. "Shared me and that was fine."

She wanted to throw up. The information that the brothers shared didn't bother her. She'd experienced it and loved every second, but hadn't wanted to be passed around among clients.

"That's enough." Nathan stood and offered his hand to Darinda. "We're leaving."

She slipped her skirt into place and hopped to her feet. She accepted his hand, not sure what else to do, but comply.

"That's it. Run away." Lola laughed. "You're not big-shot billionaires. You could have anyone. Find someone better and cough her up."

Why were they allowing the clients to talk to them this way? To insult them?

"Goodbye." Nick led the way out of the restaurant. Nathan and Darinda followed. Nick shook his head. "I can't believe it."

Darinda rushed to keep up. She wasn't sure what had happened. "Is this how they all conduct business?"

"I've had enough of this shit." Nathan opened the car door. "In."

"Yes, sir." She complied and scooted into the vehicle.

"The nerve of that bastard. I believe it because I just heard it, but God fucking damn it." Nathan slammed the door behind him and shook his head. "You'd think we've never had a business meeting. Like we're fucking green lawyers. Like we deserve disrespect."

She folded her hands together on her lap. "Why did they act that way?" She'd probably spoken out of turn, but she had to ask. "What's going on?" She'd signed on to be their date and she'd been referred to as their girlfriend and partner. What if she didn't want to be either? What if she'd like to be just another worker? She didn't, but she'd like the chance to decide. Going along with them wasn't supposed to get this complicated.

"Sweetheart?" Nathan tipped his head. "Speak up. What's wrong? You're pale."

She shook her head. "I'm sorry, but good God. I was just offered up as a commodity. I didn't ask for that to happen. I just wanted to go out."

"I know that's what you wanted." Nick sighed. "You're upset?"

"Upset?" she spat. "I'm livid."

"You have the right," Nathan said. "We didn't expect that to happen."

"I'm sure you didn't." She tensed and balled her hands. "You need to be honest with me and tell me exactly what you expect. Lay it all out and give me the chance to figure out if this is what I want and if I don't, then I have the option to ask questions. I don't like being used or surprised this way. It's not the sweet gesture you think it is."

"I know it's not." Nathan held on to her fist, caressing her knuckles. "We weren't trying to hurt you, but we've screwed up. Nick?"

"We owe you the truth, the unvarnished version. The story isn't pretty and you won't like everything you're about to hear. We'll tell you, but it won't be a happy ending—not all the way. It's up to you to say no. It'll hurt, but we can accept that." Nick curled his fingers under her chin. "Are you sure you want to go on this ride with us? I'll tell you whatever you want to know. Nathan will, too."

She should turn them down, but she had to know and have the chance to do just that if that's what she felt should happen. She'd developed feelings for them long before she'd been taken as their girl. She didn't want their money, but she needed their love, respect and honesty. She needed to be with them—good or bad. "I do."

Chapter Ten

Nathan bit back a groan. He hadn't wanted to discuss this. Never wanted to revisit their past, but she deserved to know. If she was going to be with them, she needed to know.

"When we were younger, our father gave us money. A hundred grand each. We were supposed to use that money to make more. He never told us how, just do it," Nick said. "We never should've been loose with that much cash."

"No," Nathan said. "But he did."

"And you're the one who gave us the direction for it." Nick nodded to Nathan. "If it wasn't for him, I'd have blown it all in a year."

Her eyes widened. "On what?"

"Stupid shit." Nick shrugged. "Cars, girls... I was seventeen."

"You got that much at seventeen?" She gasped. "All I got was a sleeping bag and the threat to keep my mouth shut so no one would know my dirty old uncle was hitting on me."

Nathan gritted his teeth. He should've known she'd been through something. He'd thought they'd done a thorough check on her. If he ever ran into this uncle, he'd make sure the man never saw the light of day.

"Nate got us to put the money aside and finish college. He made sure we got our law degrees," Nick said. "I hated every second. The man fucking kicked my ass during the bar."

"It was that or bust." He'd been stern about getting through so they'd be able to make money for themselves later. "We survived and now we've got the firm."

"Only the biggest in the state." Darinda grinned and squirmed in her seat. "I'm proud of what you've accomplished."

"Thank you." Nick winked. "But our father didn't give us that money out of goodness. It was insurance money."

"Our mother passed when we were seven and eight," Nathan said. "She tried her best with us, but Dad didn't have any discipline. Not for us or himself. He wanted to be happy again and did everything he could to make that happen. Women, drugs, blowing money…he did it. We watched and Nick thought he wanted to be like Dad. I didn't. I wanted to get out."

"It took lots of time. We've made enemies and accepted some deals that weren't great. They paid well, but in hindsight, it wasn't smart. We used that money to build up our firm," Nick said. "We played fast and loose with dates, with some money and didn't behave like gentlemen."

"Our father passed when we opened this building, but he wasn't happy. Never had been since Mom passed." Nathan pointed to the window. "We're at the wharf." They hadn't made a plan for where they'd go, but he'd like ice cream. He'd love to lick it off every inch of her skin too.

"Let's go to Gio's," Nick said. "Come on." He left the car first, not bothering to close the door behind him.

Darinda met his gaze for a moment, then scooted out after him.

Nathan kept up, not wanting to be left out.

"Gio's?" Darinda beamed. "In this? They won't let us in."

"They will." Nick shook his head. "You underestimate us. I'll make sure we're given the proper treatment."

Nathan held back and stood with Darinda. He shrugged out of his jacket and draped it around her shoulders. "Chilly?"

"No." She leaned into him. "This is so crazy to be out on the pier in this dress. No one's looking at us, but it feels so strange."

"It is." He waited as Nick returned with three dishes of ice cream. "No tables?"

"Not when it's warm enough to watch the water and be outside." Nick offered them the dishes. "I got everyone the special. Apricot swirl."

With Darinda between them, Nathan joined his brother at the railing and ate the ice cream. The special was good. The taste melted on his tongue and the slight heat added to the flavor. "Is there pepper in this?"

"A hint of jalapeño." Nick nodded. "It's a good kick."

"It's delicious." Darinda laughed, then glanced over her shoulder and the sound stopped. "Shit."

"What's wrong?" Nathan tried to figure out what she'd seen. "What's wrong?"

"Chloe's here." Darinda turned her back to the walkway. "She saw me and she didn't look happy."

"Don't ever hide." Nathan rubbed her back with his free hand. "Never be ashamed of that. You're our treasure."

Darinda turned and the blush deepened on her cheeks. "She's angry."

"So?" Nick finished his ice cream. "I'm sure she is."

"She's crushed on you both."

"She's not our type," Nathan replied. "You are." Why couldn't she see that?

"She'll be pissed when I see her Monday at our desks."

"Nah." Nick tossed his bowl and spoon into the recycling bin. "You're not going back to your desk."

"I'm not?"

Nathan finished his ice cream. "You're the one we chose and you're staying with us. You're not going back to the secretary pool."

"We've opened our world to you, Dar. That's not something to ignore. She wasn't interested in being with us. She just saw the money." Nick opened the door for them.

"Oh." Darinda settled on the seat and folded her hands on her lap.

Nathan entered the car first. "This isn't a temporary situation. We don't pick women at random." *Not any longer.* "We've had our eye on you and saw how you were with the clients. We've seen how you react outside of the club and danced with you. We've been with you in public and you handled the situation with Greene pretty well. Some wouldn't have been so strong. Because you've become exactly what we wanted — were all along — you're about to get everything you've ever wanted."

"I am?" She shook her head. "Guys." She held up her hands and blushed from her hairline to her chest.

Nick joined them in the car. "And this is why we've chosen you."

The adorable reaction and her honesty were more than enough. Nathan couldn't wait to get her home and fuck her in their bed, in the playroom, hold her between them and delight in her. He craved Darinda. Had since he'd first seen her. Now he'd be able to hold her.

He barely registered the car ride home as his thoughts turned to the clients. Greene had always been difficult, but nothing like tonight. On one hand, he didn't blame Greene for making a comment. Darinda was beautiful and she seemed to shimmer between them. She came alive with them. He couldn't wait to get her upstairs to fuck her again and bind her hands while he stood behind her as his brother fucked her mouth.

He and Nick could do that. She belonged to them.

She didn't belong to Greene and the raging inappropriateness of the comments annoyed him. How could Greene be so foolish? A pretty woman made him lose his senses?

Nathan could understand that. He'd fallen headlong for Darinda. But how dare they come on to her in front of the lawyers?

The car stopped and Nick exited first. Darinda followed him, but Nathan lagged back. He needed a few moments to settle down. Sure, he wanted to fuck her, but he didn't want to head into the playroom with a head of steam in a bad way.

"Nate?" Nick frowned as they entered the elevator. "What's wrong?"

"Go ahead. I'll take the next one. I need a moment." He waited as the doors closed. The other set of doors opened and he stepped into the second car. With the exception of his brother, he hadn't had anyone in his life he wanted to protect. His mother hadn't cared. She'd died and he'd never found out the real reason she'd passed away. His father had made him strong, but had damn near abandoned him and Nick to chase women. Now he was gone, too.

He rode up to the penthouse in silence and tried to rid his mind of the frustration. The best cure would be Darinda between him and Nick. When the doors opened, he stepped into the space and groaned.

Some clients didn't understand boundaries.

Just because a beautiful woman was in the room didn't mean she should be hit on or sexually assaulted.

"Nate?"

He tensed. Darinda. When he glanced over his shoulder, she stood in the doorway to the steps, barefoot and still wearing Nick's jacket. He'd never seen a more beautiful woman in his life. "Sweetheart."

"Not Naughty Girl?" She cocked her head. "Are you okay?"

He needed private time and looked forward to his moments to calm down, but seeing her standing there...he couldn't tell her no. "I'm fine." A lie, but he didn't care.

"You're angry."

"I am."

"Then you're not fine." She inched up to him and threaded her arms around his waist. "Can I help?"

He should argue and push her away, but didn't. He'd always been so picky, but what for? Now that he had who he wanted, he should take and delight in her. He smoothed his hands along her back. "You can." She smelled good and sweet. She felt even better in his arms — so soft and comforting. He could get used to this.

"Better?" she murmured.

He nuzzled her hair. "How do you make me feel ten feet tall and bulletproof when I'm not?"

"I don't know." She tipped her head to meet his gaze. "But I'll keep trying."

"You should." He held her. The anger was still there, but he wasn't so frustrated. "I hate when clients think they have the right to make comments, then act inappropriately and get upset when we decline to represent. My brother and I are particular about our clientele."

"I know you are." She tucked her hands into his back pockets. "But they believe that since they're paying you, you should do what they want. They can speak up because they feel they're in charge."

"That's normally true. Make the client happy, but things have changed. If my brother and I don't believe the client is in our best interest, then we reserve the right to turn them down. I'm not working with someone uncooperative."

"You shouldn't have to." She nodded. "I saw that with billing and coding. Every so often, I'd have to refer someone to the complaints department and they were rotten when that happened. I always wondered if the clients who were sweet or at least understanding got better treatment. I mean, we'd have some we had to deal with that were so nice and I could tell they were in a bad place, but needed some help. They're the ones my heart went out to."

"I'm sure they did." He had no true idea at the moment, but he tended to work with those who had a better attitude. He curled his fingers under her chin. She had so much wisdom for someone so young. "Are you happy?"

"Me?" She grinned and shook her head. "I am, but this is still unreal."

"I know, but I meant concerning dinner. That wasn't right. We subjected you to the fire and unfortunately, it got prickly." He regretted having her accompany them, but then again, he found out just who Greene could be, so it wasn't a total loss.

"That was nothing, really." She shrugged. "I get worse at the clubs. If I show up in something racy, then people come out of the woodwork to make a comment. I've been grabbed, pinched, poked, kissed without permission, nearly raped, spanked and groped. If I spoke up, then I was the bad one. I hated it, but it came with the territory."

"That's shit." He wanted to eviscerate every one of the men who'd misbehaved.

"I wasn't above kneeing someone. Don't touch me without permission." She blushed. "The bondage clubs were different, but you know that."

"I do." He squeezed her ass. "Is that permitted?"

She grinned. "It is — with or without the money and status. I don't need that."

"I know you don't." Which was why she was perfect for them. He couldn't see his life without her, even so quickly. "I want you to play with us tonight."

"You do?" She batted her lashes. "I hoped you'd ask."

"You know I will." He swatted her backside. "We need to negotiate, but I want you in our room and bed tonight."

"I thought I had the penthouse downstairs." She frowned. "I don't want it if I could stay with you instead."

"Sweetheart, you were never really staying downstairs, but the penthouses are connected — as you found out." He brushed a lock of her hair from her face. "You were always supposed to be up here with us."

"Oh." She blushed again. "I thought I trespassed."

"Never." He toyed with that lock of her hair. A thought occurred to him. He wanted to ask her directly about Suzy. "Do you know a Suzette LeFarge?"

She frowned again, crinkling her pretty face. "No."

"Tall, blonde, slender..." He barely remembered what she looked like because Darinda was all he saw. "Brown eyes, mole on her cheek, probably rather forward and demanding. Could be a bit on the flashy side. She's barred from the office."

She walked her fingers down his chest. "Wait." She pointed to him. "She came into the office — same general description — last week. Barged right in and came to the back where we are. Said she wasn't leaving until she talked to Nick. Was that her?"

So she'd been there? And he hadn't known. *Interesting. Where was the footage of that?* He and Nick would have to do some looking. "Could be. What happened?"

Darinda shrugged. "Mostly she waved her purse around, pointed at everyone and shouted. Said she wasn't leaving until she talked to Nick and the fucker owed her money." Her eyes widened and her lips formed an O. "I'm sorry."

"Don't sweat it." He'd punish her foul mouth later.

"I didn't know she wasn't supposed to be there. If I had, I would've alerted security to remove her." She tensed and squirmed. "I thought you knew her and she was just angry."

"Out of control." He sighed. Nick would blow a gasket when he found out. He'd say something before the scene, but after, when she slept, they'd go on a mission to find the fucking footage. The team know better than to let Suzy onto the property. If there was a breach or mole, as he'd suspected, then he wanted to know…yesterday.

"Are you sure I was okay?" She tensed again and balled her hand on his chest. "I'm sorry."

"Don't be." He brushed his thumb across her bottom lip. "Do you want to play?"

"What do you have in mind?" Her eyes lit up and a smile curled on her lips. "Do we need Nick?"

"Of course we do." None of this would happen without his brother. "First, I want you to meet us downstairs in the playroom. Wear your panties and the garter hose, along with your heels, but nothing else. Pull your hair back and wait on the bed. Nick and I will be down shortly."

"What about the lady who helped dress me? I don't want her to be in the way or get into trouble."

"She's busy and won't interfere." At least she'd asked about her. "You'll be fine."

"Yes, sir." She didn't pull away.

He appreciated her staying close and kissed her hard. He wanted to drown in her kiss. Wanted to sip from her forever. She scrambled his brains and made him fly. He swatted her ass. "Go," he said, breaking the kiss. "You know what you need to do. We'll paddle your backside and bind you, then fuck you senseless. You'll love every second."

"I know I will." She yelped as he slapped her butt again, then scurried away.

He watched her go and grinned from ear to ear. She would be the death of him, but he didn't care. He needed her.

A moment later, Nick strode into the room. "You okay?"

"I am." He faced his brother. "We have a girl waiting for us."

"We do."

He held up his hand. "First, Suzy was at the office. She got inside."

Nick's eyes flashed. "You're kidding."

"Darinda didn't know that's who she was, but she remembered the outrage. Suzy was here and she threw a fit downstairs. I know damn well we warned the team and I'm certain you and I didn't see the footage of her being there. The team knows we're to be notified and the film should be given to us right away. They also know heads will roll now that I've been informed she was here. There have to be other witnesses and the footage should be somewhere."

"We will get to the bottom of this." The muscle in Nick's jaw clenched. "Pisses me off."

"Then we'll do something fun to relax before we handle this." He leveled his gaze at his brother.

"She's waiting?"

"You bet she is."

Chapter Eleven

Darinda stripped out of her dress and left the garment on the overstuffed chair in the bedroom. She wasn't much for wearing shoes in the house—or penthouse—but they'd asked her to don the pumps. She located the garter stockings in the drawer, then removed her panties long enough to slide the delicate garment over her legs. The silk tickled her skin as she adjusted the stockings, then stepped into the panties again. The cool air caressed her chest and her nipples beaded. Soon, she'd have Nick and Nathan's hands on her again. She'd be cherished, while being given the most exquisitely painful pleasure.

She stood and smoothed her lingerie into place, then pulled her hair into an elastic before making her way back to the bed. They'd told her to sit and wait for them.

Her thoughts turned to the incident with the clients. She'd kept her head down, but she'd paid attention. How could she have missed the screaming and cursing? She'd half expected to hear gunfire or something more drastic for Suzy to make her point.

She understood what Suzy saw in them. Nick and Nathan were good men. Demanding, but controlled and sweet. When they chose someone, they cared for them completely. She'd bet Suzy wanted in on the money, too. The possibilities. Being with them meant access to money, activities, people. Who wouldn't want that?

Not Darinda.

She loved clubbing, but preferred to stick to the comfort of her favorite places. Money was good, but only as long as it got her into the club. The rest? Didn't matter.

"Naughty girl?" Nathan walked into the room first.

She gasped at the sight of him. He wore his silk shirt open to the fourth button and his tie was gone. His pants clung to his hips and he'd gone barefoot. As he unhooked his cufflinks, he left the jewelry on her dresser. He held his hand out to her.

"Are you ready?"

She nodded. "I am, sir."

"We'll wait for Nick, but we're going to negotiate first." Nathan helped her to her feet. "You're ours, but we're a team."

She liked hearing that. But she liked them. No, maybe she even loved them. She'd been in love with them for so long and never expected she'd ever be with them.

A moment later, Nick ambled into the space. Like his brother, his shirt hung open and he wore no socks. He'd stuck his hands into his pockets. Something jangled, but she wasn't sure what.

"You can object and are expected to speak." Nick rounded her. "You're delicious tonight."

"Am I?" She bowed her head, not sure what else to do. "Thank you, sir."

"Do you want to know what else we'd like to do tonight?" Nathan asked. "What we have in store for you?"

"I do." She stared at her stocking-clad feet.

"Tonight, we're taking you to the playroom. You will be ours. We plan to use your body and satisfy your senses. To make you scream and cry out," Nathan said. "You will submit to us and we will bring you pleasure beyond measure."

"Yes, sir."

"You will call us sir. You're expected to show enjoyment." Nick caressed her arm. "We will use nipple clips on you, cuffs, a blindfold and will both use you."

"Do you accept? Object? Have input?" Nathan asked. "You're in control."

She'd never been told that. She paused before speaking and didn't bother to look up. "I would like all of that."

"Louder." Nick caressed her back. "Naughty girl?"

"I would like all of that," she said, her voice strong. "My safe word is 'ghost'. I don't wish to use it."

"You trust us to give you pleasure, to care for you, punish you, but also make you fly, all while treasuring you?" Nathan asked. He curled his fingers under her chin, forcing her to look him in the eye. "Girl?"

"I trust you." She met his gaze. "I know you both will."

"Are you ready?" Nick asked.

"I am." She accepted his gentle nudge forward and walked with both men to the playroom. The warmth in the space welcomed her. Her nipples beaded and cream slicked her pussy in anticipation.

Nathan led her to a bondage table. "Up." He patted the leather. "You may use your safe word at any time."

"Thank you, sir." She crawled onto the low table on her hands and knees. Excitement surged through her. She detected the scent of sandalwood in the air. Heat caressed her body as Nathan stood before her. Nick was out of sight, but she knew where he stood because he removed her pants, one side at a time. She swore the click was the sound of scissors.

Such a waste, cutting perfectly good, expensive panties from her body. But the decadent act also intrigued her.

Nathan knelt before her and held up a pair of cuffs, metal and noisy as he moved. The cuffs weren't fixed together—rather in two separate pieces. He snapped one cuff around each of her wrists, allowing her to move. As she perched before him, he also caressed her breasts. Within seconds, the bra was removed from her body. By Nick? She believed so. Her skin prickled and she wanted to squirm. Instead, she focused on Nathan.

Nathan caressed, then pulled and pinched her nipples. She gasped, loving the rough treatment. "Thank you, sir."

"Good girl." He pulled a nipple clip from his pocket. The shiny metal caught the light.

She gasped again. The bite of the clip and the pull on her skin added to her pleasure. She dug her toes into the leather and moaned.

"Such a good girl." Nick kissed the swell of her hip.

Before she could process the pain spiraling through her other nipple as Nathan affixed the second clip, a loud crack split the air and a sting exploded across her backside. A spanking. They hadn't told her they'd swat her, but she didn't care. She loved a good spanking and knew damn well they'd seen her play at the club.

"Thank you, sir, may I have another?" she asked and panted. "Oh God."

Nathan kissed her before he stood. He unzipped his trousers and shoved the soft material to his ankles. His cock bobbed before her. The tip glistened with pre-cum. He didn't touch himself, but instead rocked on the balls of his feet. "What do you want?"

"You, sir." She leaned forward and opened her mouth, needy to make him happy. When he rocked toward her, she flicked her tongue across the blunt head.

"Yes, baby." He threaded his fingers into her hair and guided her to his dick. She swallowed him greedily, brushing her nose in his thick curls.

She admired his body, what she saw of it. So strong and hard, but soft. He'd protect her. He'd make sure she had a place to be and no one would hurt her again.

She bobbed her head, taking him deep before nearly allowing him free again.

"God, that feels good." He tugged lightly on her hair.

The combination of pressure on her head, his cock overwhelming her and the pain of the clips on her nipples turned her senses inside out.

"She needs some extra pretties." Nick stroked her belly.

A moment later, the teeth biting into her nipples dug in more. She yelped around Nathan's cock. She didn't have to look down to know what he'd done. He'd added something to the clips for a bit of heaviness.

"Beautiful." Nick stroked her stomach again. "You love being used this way."

She wanted to answer him, but it was impossible with a mouthful of Nathan. She embraced the sensations all over her body and moaned. Within seconds, she built into a steady rhythm. If Nick spanked her again, she'd come.

Nick grasped her hips. "I love the way her ass shimmers. So pink and pretty." He spanked her again.

She yelped. She needed to come. Right now.

"Don't you dare finish," Nick said. He spanked her again. "Not until I'm inside you."

She glanced up at Nathan and he grinned. She loved pleasing him. Having Nick in her pussy would be better. She'd have everything she wanted.

"Pretty, with my cock between your lips." Nathan rocked faster. "Want to mark you as ours forever."

She'd love that. She flattened her tongue and swallowed him to the root again. The cuffs weighed heavy on her wrists, but she didn't care. All she saw was Nathan and felt both him and his brother.

"I want in." Nick stopped spanking her.

The silence enveloped her as Nathan stopped moving. She listened and the screech of a zipper split the air. A smile curled stronger on Nathan's lips. He began to thrust again, fucking her mouth and pushing her toward the edge. She breathed in the scent of his cologne and basked in the tickle of his curls on her skin. She dug her fingers into the leather, trying to hold on. Her head swam. One more thrust and she'd go right over the edge.

"My turn." Nick grasped her hips.

As she plunged down onto Nathan's cock, Nick pushed into her body. The exquisite pressure added to her desire. He had enough girth to please and knew how to make her scream. She groaned around Nathan's dick. In seconds, he and his brother worked into a steady rhythm, playing her body.

She had no objections. No desire to stop this. Rather she wanted to keep going. To topple over the edge and experience bliss. She'd never known this kind of headiness.

"Don't you dare come until we do." Nick swatted her again. "So tight and needy for me. Love it."

"Made for us." Nathan tipped his head back. He growled as he increased his speed. He pulled harder on her hair.

She loved the rough treatment. Her head swam again. She could get lost in this feeling forever. She was their instrument. Their toy. To dress up, pamper, use and protect. She'd do what they wanted because this was where she needed to be. These men consumed her thoughts. Consumed her feelings.

She couldn't stop this moment if she tried. Not that she wanted to. She couldn't wait for the next moment, the next time with them and this one hadn't even ended.

"Fuck." Nathan let go of her hair and palmed her head. "I'm there." He shivered.

"Close, too." Nick surged into her. "Won't be long now."

She embraced both men's excitement. She'd done this. She'd made them happy. Her body, her soul, her abilities had pleased them. She rocked between them, experiencing them both.

Nathan shivered again and surged deep into her mouth. "Fuck me." He came hard and curled over her. Cum slid down her throat. Instead of pulling back or letting him slip free, she swallowed everything he gave her. Taking him in pushed her closer to her own climax.

Nick's movements turned feral and he slammed into her. "Yes." He said nothing else as he filled her to the hilt. His cock throbbed. He swatted her ass. "Come for us. Now."

She didn't need the command to know what to do. Her control had held by a tiny thread. Now, she could let go. She shuddered from head to toe. The clips and weights jingled as she moved. The pain evaporated. Nothing but pleasure swept over her. She cried out as she came.

Everything seemed to melt away around her. Nothing else mattered but Nathan and Nick.

"Fuck, that's beautiful." Nathan slipped from her mouth and kicked out of his trousers. He kept the shirt on, then released the cuffs around her wrists.

"Sure is." Nick withdrew. He slid his arms around her waist, supporting her.

While Nick held her, Nathan removed the clips. Nick gathered her in his arms, then carried her to the couch. He said nothing as he curled her to his chest.

She tucked into him, wishing Nick and Nathan both could hold her. She rested her head on Nick's shoulder. Nathan joined them on the couch.

"Our girl." Nick continued to pet her hair. "Rest."

She wasn't going to argue with him. Her limbs refused to cooperate and her thoughts were a mess. She closed her eyes. A whimper lodged in her throat.

"How do you feel?" Nathan stroked her cheek. "Babe?"

She opened her eyes and gazed at the man she loved. Both men. She'd fantasized over Nick and Nathan when she'd been hired at the firm. Now that she'd been with them twice, she'd begun to fall in love with them.

"Sweetheart?" Nathan tipped his head. "Rest."

"I will," she managed.

"Happy?" Nick asked.

"I am." She sighed. Her worries and cares were gone. She'd found a home with them. "Are you going to keep me?"

Nathan chuckled. "We are."

"Do you want to be kept?" Nick winked. "We weren't planning on letting you go."

"I do." She snuggled into him, ready to sleep.

Nathan stood. "Let's take her to bed. We all need rest and I don't want to be without her."

She didn't mind that he'd spoken about her like she wasn't there. She allowed Nick to carry her out of the room to the bedroom on the upper floor. Once there, Nick and Nathan stripped her to nude. She crawled between the sheets and settled. Sleep filled her mind. She swore she'd crash in seconds.

Nick joined her on the left and Nathan on the right.

She grinned as she closed her eyes. She pressed her belly to Nick's backside and Nathan pressed into her ass, situating his dick between her ass cheeks. She'd never been anywhere more perfect or more loved in her life.

For once, she had exactly what she wanted.

What she needed.

* * * *

Darinda spent the next few days with her men, but also on her own. While they worked, she had free rein of the building and her choice of whatever she wanted. She could finish her college courses, could have any food she desired, clothes, shoes, jewelry...

For a kid who'd been thrown out of her own home and forced to live on her wits, this was the life. Her friends back home would never recognize her.

She'd been given her own credit card to shop however she pleased, as long as she took a bodyguard. Nick and Nathan demanded to go wherever she did, but sometimes that wasn't possible.

She left the penthouse with her guard in tow and had Nick and Nathan's driver take her to the boutiques. She'd only dreamed of shopping there when she'd been a club kid. Now she could afford to buy whatever she pleased.

Her phone rang and she jerked. Nick and Nathan didn't call her. They sent texts or simply showed up. She loved the surprise visits. But this wasn't Nick or Nathan calling. She groaned and checked the ID.

Neurfman Legal Services

She frowned. What did they want with her? She swiped and answered. A thought occurred to her. Her parents were probably in trouble and demanding cash to get out of trouble.

"This is the Neurfman Legal Services, Alice speaking. Hello, Ms. Mace. I've been hoping to hear from you," Alice said. "I'm calling on behalf of Attorney Cutloff. We've tried to contact you for the last two days. You've inherited money from your father's insurance policy and you need to collect it in person."

"Wait." She massaged her forehead. "What?" Her mother should be given the money first.

"According to your father's wishes, you're the only beneficiary for his insurance policies. He'd made the

NLS firm his power of attorney and the balance of his estate has been used to pay his medical expenses," Alice said. "I'd like to discuss this with you in person. Are you available this afternoon?"

"I'm across the state." She stared at the back of the front seat. Shock washed over her. Power of attorney, father's estate. None of it made sense. "Where's my mother?"

"Ms. Mace, she's deceased."

She swore the ground collapsed beneath her. "Deceased?"

"It would be much better to explain this in person."

"I can be there this afternoon, but I'd like an explanation now." She gestured to the guard. "We need to get to Cattlesville, Ohio. I need to speak to the Neurfman Legal Services today."

"I'll let the bosses know." The guard nodded once.

"No." She held up her hand. "Not yet." She hated not telling Nick and Nathan, but this was too complicated and messy. Besides, they'd done a background check on her. They had to know how fucked up her life had been.

Right now, she had to get across the state to sort out the problems. She turned her attention back to the phone. "I'm sorry, Alice. I was making arrangements to be there this afternoon." By three, if she guessed correctly. "Please tell me what happened." She'd deal later with her men and the repercussions of not talking to them sooner.

"As you know, your father has battled substance abuse for the last dozen years," Alice said. "Your mother was clean, but he's struggled."

"It's been longer than years." She massaged her forehead again. "Go on."

"In one of his bouts with rehab, your father enlisted the help of NLS to get his affairs in order. To that end, he made you — after his estate — the sole beneficiary of his insurance policies. Your mother, though clean, never gave up on him. She was with him when he passed away."

"At the hospital?" She didn't understand.

"There was an accident," Alice said. "Your mother was driving him to the hospital after an overdose. While en route, a drunk driver struck her. She was killed and brought to the hospital. The medical examiner believes he died from the overdose and on account of the crash because medical attention wasn't given to him in time. Would you like to sue the driver? We can get that going for you if you'd like."

"No." A lawsuit wouldn't bring her parents back or get them clean. She closed her eyes. She'd never be able to face Nick and Nathan now. Her past was so fucked up. She wasn't worthy of them. Just a poser. Someone who looked like they wanted Nick and Nathan's money.

Fuck.

"You're on your way, Ms. Mace?" Alice asked. "The sum of money isn't large, but it's yours and it's stipulated you sign for it in person."

She had little choice. This had to be done. Nick and Nathan would be livid, and probably even more so because she should have legal representation for this meeting but there wasn't time. "I'll be there."

And she'd take responsibility for her actions later.

Just don't let them hate me.

136

Chapter Twelve

Nick's phone buzzed in his pocket. He hated checking the device while working, but he and Nathan had yet another client meeting. He stepped out of the conference room and withdrew the phone. If his personal device was making noise, then something was wrong with Darinda. Nathan was in the conference with him and few others had the private number. He'd bet Darinda didn't even know she'd been given such classified information.

He swiped the screen to retrieve the text. Hopefully something nude from Darinda. Not a text and not from Darinda. From Mario.

Fuck.

Mario was the best guard they had, but he wasn't much for talking. Mario equaled action. If he'd texted, there was trouble. He read the message.

Heading to Cattlesville with Darinda. Said she needs to speak with a lawyer. Won't tell me what for. Will notify on arrival and have turned on GPS so can be tracked.

Cattlesville? He leaned on the wall and read the text a third time. He'd read her files. She'd grown up in Cattlesville, but hadn't been back in ages. It wasn't a big town, but enough to support a hospital. He frowned.

A moment later, the door opened and Nathan joined him in the corridor. "What's wrong?"

"Huh?" He stared at his brother. What in the hell would she have gone to Cattlesville for without telling them and why in such a hurry?

"The Kennedys have left and they've hired the firm. They've decided we can get them the best investment deal and will be cutthroat when it comes to buying those horse farms." Nathan folded his arms. "What's upsetting you? Darinda? Where is she? Is she okay?"

"She's on her way to Cattlesville." He shoved the phone into Nathan's hands. "I'm guessing he's texted you, too, but she's gone."

"Whoa." Nathan handed the phone back. "So that's what the text means."

"She's gone."

"Don't jump to conclusions." Nathan matched Nick's stance. "There's a good reason."

"I bet there is. She's run away. She's not happy and I'm pissed. Spends money, doesn't tell us where she's going and runs the fuck away. I can't see straight." He'd been angry before, but not like this. How could she leave them? They'd become a package deal. She was their third.

"You're getting way too wound up about this," Nathan said. "It's not that dire."

"Not that fucking dire? Are you serious?" He glared at his brother. "This is bullshit."

"Okay. You need to breathe."

Only his brother could say that to him and not send him into a blind rage. He gritted his teeth and fought to gather his anger back into the box.

"Now, I personally researched her. I know her background. I'm not thrilled she just up and left without so much as a word, but I don't think it's as dire as you believe. Her family is in Cattlesville. Her parents are both junkies and it wouldn't surprise me if one of them is either dying or has died. When our father passed, we went right there and hadn't seen him in years. It's something you do, and she's decided to do that. I can't fault her for going home."

His brother made sense, but that didn't make this easier. "Sure."

"And the text mentions she's speaking to a lawyer. She's not going to find one without us. I'm guessing she's been summoned. Should she have brought us along? Yes, because we can help her, but she must've believed she had to do this on her own. Am I hurt that she didn't tell us? I am. Very much so. I thought she trusted us. But this may have been too quickly unfolding and there's a chance she just wasn't prepared." Nathan sighed. "I'm also hurt because I love her. I never thought I'd fall in love again, but I have."

He stared at his brother. He hadn't thought he'd hear Nathan say that. "You have?" He'd fallen for her, too.

"I have. I want to keep her, and not just because we've said we want her. I'm ready to make it permanent. We've waited too long for this." Nathan pulled his own phone out. "We'd talked about this before, but I think we need to do this." He showed his brother a drawing on the phone.

He stared at the tattoo idea he and Nathan had tossed around for years. Seeing it now, he liked the design. "We should do it. I'll add to mine and you get one."

"We should, but after we discuss things with her. We've been too good at letting anyone who disappoints us simply fall out of our lives. We can't do that with her. If she means as much to us as we claim she does, then we need to hear her out. We also need to give her space to handle this problem," Nathan said. "But that doesn't mean we can't do our own checking and use Mario. He's not there just to look pretty."

Nick snorted. Mario was built like a brick wall and looked like he'd collided with one a few times. He wasn't pretty, but rather rugged. Also not Nick's type. He'd guess not Darinda's, either. "Okay."

"We give her a little while, but we'll message Mario in the meantime to discern what's going on." Nathan shoved his phone into his pocket. "Now, we have a bigger issue to handle."

"Where to get the ink?" Nick sighed and relaxed. He had to trust Darinda and that was the hardest part. He'd been burned in the past and wasn't sure he could trust, but if it was possible, then she'd be the one.

"No, our ex has shown up." Nathan nodded to the conference room. "And I know who's been giving her information."

Nick dragged Nathan down to their personal office, out of sight of any other workers. He waited until the door was shut and locked. If there was indeed a mole, then he wanted that information as private as possible. "Who?"

"Gert."

"No." He shook his head. "She's been the best secretary we've ever had, and loyal."

"Loyal isn't the word I'd use," Nathan said. "She's good at keeping some secrets and she's great with filing, but she's been talking to Suzy. I caught the surveillance of them. I also happened to uncover their friendship. It's very much on the down-low, but it's there."

God damn it. Nick wanted to punch something. To dismantle anything he could find. "Why would she do that to us?"

"I'm guessing she's going to try to get money. We pay her well, but if she can milk the billionaires for more...just like Suzy...then it's worth a shot. I'm guessing they saw that we've been lavishing attention on Darinda and wanted in on it," Nathan said. "In Suzy's case, again."

"You're right." They'd given Darinda everything she'd ever wanted and had never done that with Suzy. Gert had been their best employee, but wasn't involved in everything. She didn't even have access to their personnel files. "When do you think she's making her move?"

"As soon as she can. Probably why Suzy's here."

He held up one hand. "Think that's why Darinda was sent to the lawyer?" He hated to think their ex would be that terrible, but he wouldn't be surprised.

"No. It's not her style. Suzy's smart and Gert is, too, but I could see them running a con together." Nathan rested his fingers in his pockets. "With Darinda, we'll talk to her once she's back. I'll let Mario know to tell her we're available when she needs us. I have no doubt she can handle this situation on her own, but she needs our help. We're behind and beside her."

"We are." Nick nodded and shifted his stance. "I'll handle Gert. You keep an eye on Darinda. We're going to fire her."

"Darinda?" Nathan's brows rose, but he chuckled. "I know who you meant."

"You do." He shook his head. "Go. I have the feeling we won't need to rescue her, but we'll have to show her we won't blow a gasket like I did when she does tell us."

"You've got it." Nathan dipped his head once. "I'll be upstairs."

"I'll go handle the other." Nick left the office and surged out to Gert's desk. She sat at the laptop, but he noticed her hands tremble. "Gert?"

"Sir." She put her hands down and faced him. "How can I help you? You've dialed down your workload?"

"We did." It was a lie, but they'd detoured much of their caseload away from her attention. "I see you've put in for a vacation." He'd seen it, but she hadn't brought up the dates or the request.

"I did." She stood. "I expect compensation for it."

"It's expected."

She stared at him for a moment, then continued. "You've been courting some interesting company and spending money rather freely. I've been quite loyal all these years and feel I should be given some consideration." She folded her arms. "She's not much more than a secretary and you've taken her into your confidence. Are you sure you should've?"

"Gert." He refused to show any emotion. He'd seen this game before, but hadn't thought she'd try to use them this way. Everyone else had—except Darinda. "What are you saying?"

"I'm saying you've given her money and I deserve some. I've cleaned up after you and that brother of yours for years. Gotten you out of trouble. Gotten rid of dates, problems. What have I been given for it? I live in a shitty apartment, drive a car that's not new and have to pay for my own clothes." She stepped up to him. "I deserve an allowance, a better apartment—maybe one in this building—and a new car, plus a better pay package."

"You do." He laced his fingers together. "And you should have it."

"I should? I knew you'd be easily persuaded." She smiled, but the grin dripped of greed. "I knew once you found a woman, you'd mellow."

"We have." But not toward her. "You're not done bargaining, are you?"

"No." She shook her head. "Suzy was treated terribly. You should give her another chance. Ditch the secretary and make up with your girlfriend. She's missing both of you, but mostly you."

"I remember." She'd given up the plan so much easier than he'd expected. He'd thought she was savvy. "Why don't we discuss that? Get your coat and we'll talk."

"We should." She gathered her belongings. "I've been thinking about the tenth floor. It's quite nice, and I've been looking at a new car. There are some wonderful sports cars out there. What do you drive?"

"We don't." He walked her out to the corridor and closed the entry to the office. "But we've got drivers."

"I'd like one. You need to take better care of your staff, starting with me." She stepped into the elevator. "I deserve better."

"You do." He rode with her to the ground floor, grateful it was only three floors down. In the lobby, he remained in the elevator car. "But I can't help you."

"You can't?" She stood in the lobby. "What are you talking about?"

He nodded once to the guards. She had some power over the guards, but not much.

"I've been a loyal employee." She yanked him into the lobby. "You need to take care of me."

"I am." He waited for the guards to approach. "Thank you for your service to the firm, but we cannot keep you on the staff. You've been given a generous severance package. You're no longer permitted to be in the building and will be removed if you try to enter the property."

"Why?" She lobbed her purse at him. "Why are you doing this?"

"Because we need employees we can trust. You've disclosed information to individuals not otherwise permitted to know. I don't care who we've welcomed into our personal lives, and who we have isn't your business. Since that's a problem for you, you'll have to find other employment."

"I will not!" She swiped at him, only to be restrained by the guards. "I'm not doing this. I'll sue."

He simply nodded. She could bring legal action, but he wasn't worried. He had the best firm on his side — his.

He waited for the guards to remove Gert. He'd have her belongings removed at once and sent a text to the staff in the office to do just that.

"There you are."

He bristled at the tone. Of all the people… When he turned on his heel, Suzy rushed up to him. "Darling." She threw her arms around him. "I've missed us."

Missed us? He wished she hadn't made the scene right by the doors. The paparazzi flashed photos of them. Why not? He and Nathan had obscene amounts of money and a paparazzi photo of them with another woman would start a bidding war. Who could get the highest amount for shutting the paparazzo up. He tried to peel her off him, but not before photos were no doubt snapped. Damn it. He tried to be careful, but she'd known when to strike.

"When are we setting the date?" She held up her left hand, highlighting an ostentatious diamond ring. "I will."

"Let's go inside." At least to the interior of the building away from the windows.

"Yes, let's." She snuggled into him. "I can't wait to make the announcement."

He guided her to the corridor leading to the parking garage behind the building. The guards could see them, but the outside world could not.

"You're going to get rid of that nasty person you're with and let Nathan have her. I'm the only one you've ever wanted and now that I know I am, I'm not going anywhere." She rested her hand on his chest. "I love that suit on you. It's so powerful."

"Yes." He managed to put space between them and thanked God he hadn't brought anything besides his phone with him. "What are you doing?"

"What? Baby." She reached for him. "Come here."

"No." He stepped out of her grasp. "You're not my girl, I'm not your baby, and I'm not taking you back.

We're done and there is a restraining order. You're not supposed to be here."

"I know that," she snapped. "But now there's photographic proof that you weren't upset by my challenging the order."

"I guarantee I don't look thrilled about it. But it's also proof you challenged the order." But he understood in an instant what she'd done. Photographic proof to use against him and hurt Darinda with... *Fuck.* He could fix this. That was his job. Fixing things. "You need to go. I've contacted security."

"I've gotten around it. Didn't my dear friend let you know?" She glared at him, then her glare turned sly. "Gertie will do anything for money."

"*Gertie* doesn't work here any longer." He pressed the panic button by the door. The silent alarm went out to the guards, who flooded the space. "And you're no longer welcome ever again," Nick said. "I've had enough."

"You can't do this to me." She struggled against the guards. "Doesn't matter. Your girlfriend will leave you because she's seen me and your little romance is blown. That's enough. If I can't be happy, you can't either."

He fixed his expression, like he did in court, and waited for her to leave. *God damn it.* He wished he hadn't fallen for her shenanigans but he'd been so busy getting rid of Gert, he'd fallen for the act.

The guards escorted her from the building and once she was out of his sight, Nick bounded to the interior, then to the elevator. He jabbed the buttons to get to the office. He wasn't sure how long Darinda had been away or when she'd return. First, he needed to speak to his brother.

The car ascended the building and his stomach lurched. Then again, it could be the lack of lunch hitting him. As the doors opened, he practically ran into the office. "Nathan?"

"Fuck." Nathan held one of the tablets. "She struck, didn't she?" He turned the tablet around, showing Nick the screen.

As he'd suspected, images of Nick and Suzy flooded the page. "They wasted no time."

"Not a second." Nathan tossed the tablet onto his desk. "Gert's gone. Everything's been cleaned out. The restraining order is the works. As for Suzy, there seems to be proof you allowed her to ignore hers, but we'll sort that out once we get Darinda back here."

"Is she coming home?" His skin itched and he shifted from one foot to the other, unable to stand still.

"Mario's making sure she returns. I've talked to her a moment and she's indeed coming back." Nathan sat on the edge of his desk. "I don't know what to do about the photos, though. She's seen them."

"How do you know?"

"Mario clued me in. Apparently, our dinner meeting date was plastered on the tabloid sites and they figured out who Darinda is. Once they figured that out, they contacted her and have ensured she'd see the photos today. We weren't careful."

He groaned. No, he and Nathan hadn't been, but they hadn't expected to get into such a jam. The other women before Darinda hadn't been someone they wanted to keep. She was. "We have a big problem."

"We can't let her go." Nathan's shoulders sagged and sadness filled his eyes. "Can't."

"I agree." They needed a plan, and fast. He drummed his fingers on the desk. "When is she due back?"

"A couple hours. Seven at the latest." Nathan stood upright. "What are you thinking?"

"I'm thinking we need to do something big and intended. Something she'll love, but that will show our love in return. We love her, right?" Nick asked. "She's the one, right?"

"She is and I know I love her." Nathan straightened a bit more. "What are you thinking?"

"We need to buy a necklace." He drummed the desk again. "We need a necklace, a lock that's permanent and a bold gesture. We've got two hours, give or take. Think we can do it?"

Nathan grinned. "For the woman we love? Yes, we can."

Nick worked through his plan, pulling the pieces together in his mind. He and Nathan could make everything work. Pictures could be explained, true love wouldn't die in the course of a day and gestures were always made to be big—especially since they had the cash to grease the wheels.

"Nick?" Nathan pocketed his keys and wallet. "Ready?"

"I'm so ready," Nick said. "She's the one and we're not letting her go. No question."

Chapter Thirteen

Darinda rode back to the penthouse and refused to look at Mario. She clutched the check, focusing her attention on it instead. Two thousand, seven hundred and forty-eight dollars and fifty-nine cents. That's all her parents were worth now. Life was only worth a couple thousand dollars. Sure, she hadn't had the best relationship with them. The estrangement was real, but that didn't make the hurt any less.

The money wasn't much, but it would afford her the chance to start over.

Again.

Tears blurred her vision. She'd never get those images out of her mind. Her phone had buzzed while she'd been at the lawyer's office, but instead of sweet messages from Nick and Nathan, she'd been sent photos of Nick tangled up with Suzy. Not just a hug between former friends, but a full-on engagement shot. Showing off her ring. Showing off the restarting of the relationship. They were engaged!

Showing off the cruelty.

Mario had insisted the images weren't real.

She knew better. Not real her ass. They looked so authentic…painfully so.

She'd thought she could trust them. Thought she could love them. She'd given them her body and her heart. The whole situation had gone way too fast. How could it not? They'd swept her off her feet and offered her so many things she'd never thought she could have. Money, access, love. But it was all a joke.

She'd been foolish to think this would all work. Foolish to believe the club kid deserved better.

As the car pulled into the underground parking area, she formulated a plan to escape. She'd head upstairs and pack up her things before the guys knew. She'd wait until they were busy, then get the hell out of there. There was always a new town to explore and a new place to attempt to put down roots. It wasn't like she'd never done this before. She'd started over twice, but now it was time to go to another state.

The images of Nick and Suzy returned to the forefront of her mind, like the scenes had been burned into her brain. Anger, hurt and fear gripped her. Anger that Nick and Nathan would be so callous as to use her. They'd seemed different. Hurt that she'd allowed herself to put her heart on the line. She'd prided herself on keeping up a wall, but the moment Nick and Nathan had made a move, she'd torn those walls down.

Mostly, though, she feared the next chapter in her life. She'd thought she'd had a handle on everything. Go to work, drool over her bosses, club at night or on the weekends…each week, rinse and repeat.

Being with her men now seemed like a wonderful, but sad dream.

The car stopped and she left the vehicle before Mario could stop her. She knew the codes and rushed to the elevator. She forced the doors to close without Mario beside her. Would he text Nick or Nathan to tell her what she'd done? No doubt.

But she'd be gone before they could intervene.

When the doors opened into her penthouse, she rushed across the space to her bedroom. She'd only spent a couple nights there without her guys. Oddly enough, it didn't feel like home. It felt cold. Unattached.

She pulled her suitcase from the closet and left the beat-up case on the bed. She hadn't brought much with her. Hell, her apartment was still in her name. The lease wasn't up for another couple months. Maybe she could hide there for a few weeks until she figured out what to do.

She tossed the few garments she'd brought with her and scooped the dingy bear she'd had since childhood into the suitcase.

The bracelets they'd given her jangled on her wrist. She removed the jewelry, then kicked out of the high-heeled shoes. She'd live with the lower-heeled ones she'd worn when she'd followed them upstairs the first time. She removed the cocktail ring and donned her original footwear.

When she left, she wanted nothing they'd given her. *Just walk away and forget everything.*

"Where are you going?" When she whipped around, Nathan stood in the bedroom doorway. "Sweetheart?"

"I'm not your sweetheart." She zipped the case shut. "What do you mean, where am I going? I'm leaving."

"Why?" He folded his arms, but didn't leave his spot.

"Why?" She snorted. How could he be so dense? He was a brilliant lawyer. He had to know what was going on. "Don't start."

"Don't?" He remained in the doorway. "You're free to leave. We've never said you were our prisoner, but before you go, we expect an explanation."

"You do?" She barely kept her frustration under control. "Nick was tangled up with that woman you said was dangerous. Showing off her engagement ring. The papers made sure I knew about it and texted me. I've been bombarded with reminders that neither one of you wants me. I did a little looking on my own and see that not only did you know I was the girl you'd danced with, but that you made it possible for me to work here. You orchestrated that. Not me working and making a difference on my own. Not me showing I'm capable. You fucking held the controls and I don't like it. You knew about my parents, knew the shit I'd gone through and you held the levers on it. I'm pissed beyond recognition and don't want to be here right now, so yeah, I'm leaving."

Nathan unfolded his arms and growled.

"See? You know it was wrong, but you did it. All of it was wrong. That's why I've got to go. I'm not staying where I'm not wanted." She picked up the case. "Bye, Nathan."

"Stop." He held up both hands. "Please?"

She halted in her tracks. He and Nick weren't ones to say please and the gesture shocked her. She held on to the case with both hands. Too late for apologies. "No." She sidestepped him and headed into the living room. Without bothering to look back, she strode right to the elevator and into the car. Her heart ached, but she refused to give either man attention. They'd done so much damage and she wasn't even sure things could be repaired.

As the door closed, she swore she heard one of them shout, but she squeezed her eyes shut. If she looked at either Nick or Nathan, she'd capitulate and right now wasn't the time to do that. She rode the elevator to the ground floor to the sidewalk. She had to get out of there.

She pulled out her phone and called Gavin. If nothing else, he'd come get her. She started walking, not bothering to look back. She wasn't foolish enough to have him pick her up at the firm. Not when Nick or Nathan could come down and try to talk her into staying. She had to be strong.

After four rings, Gavin answered. "Hey."

"Hi. Are you busy?" Her voice wobbled, despite her best attempts to stay strong. "Fuck," she muttered.

"You're crying. Where are you?"

"I'm at the Bistro Coffee shop." She'd be there in a couple minutes.

"I'm on my way."

"Stay on the phone until you get here." She wasn't ready to be alone. She fumbled with her case and crossed the street. "This sucks."

"What does?"

She heard the rattle of his keys and the hum of the car engine. "They were the masterminds of all this."

"Of what?"

She stopped inside the bistro, then headed to one of the booths. "My life. They knew about my folks, about my living situation and my job. They took care of everything. I don't have my car, I've only got about two grand to my name and I don't have a job any longer because I won't work for someone who only hired me for my body."

"Oh, honey."

"Yeah." She massaged her forehead. "I had to see the lawyers about my parents. I don't care about the money they left me. They wasted it all anyway, so it's not a huge loss to me. It's the principle of the thing. Nick and Nathan have been circling me, like sharks, watching me until I ended up at the firm. Then they used a performance review to convince me to be with them."

"That's...odd." His end of the line fuzzed with static. "I'm here." He'd driven way too fast, but fuck it.

"I should order something so it's not so unethical." A coffee or something. Not that she was hungry or thirsty.

"I'll get something." He rushed into the bistro and located her right away. "You're fine?"

"Yes." She managed to stand, but her knees buckled. "I feel ridiculous."

"Don't." He held up his hand, then walked away and returned a few moments later. "I ordered coffee. Now you haven't done anything wrong — not that you did." He picked up her suitcase.

"Thanks."

"Tell me everything. I thought you were happy with them?"

"I was." She took the case from him. "So you can carry the cups."

"Smart."

She waited with him by the counter. "Remember when we were at the club and you needed me to help you demonstrate your abilities? Turns out they were watching me."

"How'd you figure that out?"

"Cologne. They have a certain scent they wear and I detected it the first night. Then Chloe told me I had an interview at the firm. I'd only put an application in because it was a long shot and I had nothing to lose. I got the interview, then hired. It was almost too easy — because they'd orchestrated it. They danced with me at the club when we went out and they were the ones who helped me dodge the creepers trying to grab me. I said, they were sharks."

"Sounds like they're intoxicated with you and wanted to be with you. That's not totally horrible."

"No?" She waited as he accepted the cups, then strode ahead of him out of the bistro. When she reached his car, she abandoned her case and opened the door for him. "I had no say."

"Not exactly. You've always got the right to say no. No is a full sentence." He plunked the cups into the holder in the console. "You've told me that so many times."

"I did, but that's not the point." She carried the case to the trunk. "Pop it for me."

"Pushy." He did as she'd demanded. "Want help?"

"No." She pushed the case into the tight compartment, then slammed the lid. Her irritation ebbed a bit, but she still wanted to give Nick and Nathan a piece of her mind. She joined Gavin in the car and scrubbed her face with both hands.

"Okay, wait." He didn't bother to turn on the engine. "So…they held the controls on your life. They did what with your folks?"

"They manipulated everything. My parents were in trouble financially and somehow Nick and Nathan knew my folks were dying, so the guys made sure everything was handled. Nick and Nathan thought they were doing a good thing, but my parents are greedy. I bet they figured they'd get in on the financial gravy train before they cashed in — so to speak — so they honeyed up to Nick and Nathan. My folks knew what they were doing — scamming." She needed to breathe. "It's crazy and it's not even the worst of it."

"Hold up." He waggled his hand. "Wait. Holy shit, that's fucked up. And it's not the worst? What did your parents do?"

"They threw me out."

"Okay, so that's not the best thing parents can do. Mine didn't exactly spend a lot of time with me, so I get it. But honestly, they were trying to be kind, it sounds. Trying to make you happy and keep them happy. One less thing for you to have to worry about."

She stared at him. Maybe he did make sense, but the manipulation annoyed her. "Okay, then explain away the job situation."

He played with his keys and didn't speak right away. "Okay, so they saw you at the club and wanted you. Is that wholly bad? I mean, they did give you a job that paid pretty well. They didn't exactly make you stop clubbing and based on that photo you sent me of the dress you got to wear, they must really like you. I guess I don't see the big deal. Two men want to be devoted to you, give you whatever you want, and love you. That's the stuff most people would dream of."

She hated when he made sense. "Just…will you take me home?"

"I will." He shook his head, then engaged the engine. "I get why you're upset, though. You're trying to make this life happen on your own terms. You've been doing it all along and I commend you for it. Some people aren't strong enough for that."

"You might be right." She stared at her hands. "I'm just upset."

"There's nothing wrong with being that way. Like I said, I do understand. I don't like when someone else pulls the reins in on me and then tries to run my life. It's mine."

"Exactly."

"But..." He turned out of the lot and drove across town toward her apartment building. "Think about this. It's not cool that they orchestrated so much, but guys don't just do that because they're assholes. I saw how they looked at you at the club. I remember the night we were simply there and you'd allowed me to use you as my submissive arm candy for the night. That hunger wasn't just sexual. It was primal. Raw. Nick took me aside later and asked about you. Said he'd fallen for you and wanted to know how to contact you. I think they must've already known who you were, but he was truly interested."

She didn't believe him. "They want to run my life."

"Do they?"

"Uh...yeah." She folded her arms. "Aren't you listening?"

"I could ask you the same thing." He parked on the street in front of her building. "Look, they're pushy and probably heavy-handed. They've got so much money, it's not real, but they're head over heels for you."

"How do you explain that Nick got engaged?" She'd forgotten to explain that to Gavin. "Yeah, I saw the links and have been bombarded with messages asking me why I'm there when he's already with someone."

"What?" He frowned. "How...wait."

"I'm listening."

"I just need a moment to understand. What's their deal?"

She shook her head. "I don't care that they had someone else because I know I'm not that fantastic. I'm a throwaway kid who had to run away from home because my parents are shits. I like to club, be nude and I'm not in their class. It's fine."

"No, that's not fine." He grasped her hand. "First, you're not throwaway. You're a survivor. Second, you're not bad because you have kinks. It makes you human and one hell of a lot better than most people who don't understand what the fuck it's like to be true to yourself."

He made a lot of sense, even if he did annoy her. "Thanks for the ride home."

"Wait." He didn't let go. "You're not bad and you're not garbage. You're unique and they see that. I know they do. Who gives a fuck if you're not in their class bracket? Who really wants to be?"

She wanted to reply *me*, but didn't. Instead, she kept her mouth shut.

"But the engagement thing…I saw how they looked at you. Why would they get engaged to someone else? What if it's not real? Have you thought of that?" he asked. "I'm guessing it's a show."

"Maybe." That was plausible, too.

"Just give that a thought. Don't close the door on them, but give yourself some time to cool down. You're upset and hurt, which you should be, but you're also closing the door on something that's still new. I'm not saying to let them back in right now. Just give it a bit before you do, and really think about whether you want to end this or not. You might realize you're not ready to say goodbye. Not because you want the money or stuff. I know you and that's not your thing. Because you really do like them and you've got to admit, you've been more than a little in love with them all along."

She didn't want to admit he was right, but he was. "Okay."

"Give it the night? Please?"

"Are you under their spell, too?" She opened the car door. "Gav?"

"No." He chuckled and left the car as she did. "But I'm in the process of getting a new car. I hate this hunk of junk."

"I knew you would." She rested her hands on the car roof. "I just wanted to make my own way, forget my path forward and do this myself, too."

"You are." He rounded the trunk. "Tell them how you feel and hear them out, then decide. Give it a night to cool off, too. If you can see your life without them, then that's it. If you can't, then you know what you've got to do."

She nodded as he got the case out of the trunk. "Thanks, and I will." She'd give it more than one night. "I just need to cool off." Or at least have some time away from their decadence and just exist.

"It'll be okay." He hugged her. "Do you need anything else? I'm playing at the club tonight."

"No. I'd like to be alone." She sighed. Clubbing did sound fun, but she'd rather not have the noise, the questions and the reminders of her time with Nick and Nathan. "Thanks, though. Thanks for the ride, the save and being a good friend."

"Welcome. No charge." He grinned as she waved again. "You've got this."

"Thanks." She wasn't convinced. Not even close. But she had no choice. This was her life and her decision — good or bad. She'd live with the consequences.

But could she live without Nick and Nathan?

Chapter Fourteen

The next morning, Darinda stared at her ceiling. She missed the big bed, but mostly she missed the two sets of arms wrapped around her. The way they held her, the soft whispers in her ear. The tenderness.

No, she'd walked away from that.

And left her heart behind in the process.

She scrubbed her face with both hands again. She had to be strong. Nick and Nathan were manipulators. They'd pushed her. It was only right that she push back and not give in.

A knock at her door jolted her from her thoughts. She glanced at the clock. Eight in the morning. She couldn't be due at work. Turning her back on Nick and Nathan was more or less her quitting her job. They wouldn't want her as an employee. Not when she'd rejected them.

The knocking continued and she sighed. She left her bed and padded barefoot to the door. If a collection agency had tracked her down to pay one of her parents' bills, she'd scream. "Who is it?"

"Us."

She froze. She knew that voice. Nathan. What were they doing at her apartment? She had to clean. Had to...what? Find a new place to live that wasn't so shabby?

"Will you let us in?" Nathan asked. "Please?"

She should keep the lock in place, but instead, she turned the knob. She opened the door. "Hi."

"Hi." Nathan moved out of the way, letting Nick enter first. Nathan closed the door behind them. "It's good to see you."

"I just left yesterday." She sat on the arm of the sofa. "You're here. You said you wanted me to hear you out. I'm listening." Not changing her mind, but listening.

"Babe." Nick stopped short of joining her at the sofa. "Why did you go?"

"What?" This was unreal. "I don't have to explain myself. What you did was all over the internet." Besides, she'd told them yesterday.

Nathan held up his hands again. "You don't have to tell us." He perched on the coffee table, facing her. "You scared us by walking off. At least you had Mario with you yesterday, but last night you were on your own. You freaked us out because we weren't sure what was going on."

"And I don't think you told us everything." Nick leveled his gaze at her. "What's going on?"

She rolled her eyes. They expected a damn reason. She'd give them a few. "For God's sake. My parents are dead. Dad was still using and he'd overdosed and my mother was taking him to the hospital. She'd gotten clean, but when she drove him to the ER, a drunk driver hit them. Funny, the substance that nearly killed them through their own abuse — alcohol — would ultimately end their lives. Dad was strung out on pills and whatever he'd drunk himself silly on and did too much. But that was Dad. He never knew where the edge was and jumped over it all the time. Apparently, they owed too much money in too many places and the lawyers have been sorting it all out. I didn't even know they'd been killed — but I hear you did. It was in the articles I found when I went looking to figure out why you, Nick, were engaged. Yeah, I know about that."

"Sweetheart." Nathan slipped her hands into his and caressed her knuckles. "I can't imagine how losing your folks feels."

"I wasn't close to them, but it still hurts." She didn't pull away from him, despite her anger. His touch comforted her. "They died a couple weeks ago, but I wasn't notified until today. You'd think that since the tabloids knew to find me about you two, they'd have told me about my folks, but they didn't."

"We knew." Nick scooted over to the cushion beside her. "We were trying to help you."

"I know you did and it did help — them. I'm glad you took care of some of their issues and helped to get Mom clean, but Mom had to do it for herself. She wanted someone to get her out of trouble." She shifted her gaze over to Nick for a moment. "The trip started out as simply picking up a check and their ashes, but it turned into something more."

"Did you bring them with you?" Nathan asked. "We can help you inter them. Find somewhere nice for them."

"I scattered their ashes at the lake where they liked to go when they were dating." She wasn't about to mention the fact her parents had gone to that lake to shoot heroin when they were younger, too. "I scattered them, then called the cemetery in town. I'm having a pair of plates made for the memorial wall, so it's all taken care of, but I appreciate you both getting involved and making sure the plates are paid for."

"We were trying to take care of you." Nathan sat on her other side. "You had every right to go and we were out of line to get involved. It was done out of love, but we didn't tell you."

"It's fine. I was given a check for a little under three grand—which is all I have left of my parents. They didn't even give a shit about me, but I made a point to take care of them in the end. I couldn't do this with you beside me. I had to do this all on my own. Not with your help."

Nick sighed. "You did and did it well."

"I tried." She grasped Nathan's hand. He hadn't hurt her in the same way Nick had, but she wasn't ready to give either of them forgiveness. Still, she needed Nathan's strength. "That's what I did. I went, I handled it, and I'm back. What about you? What about those pictures? What am I supposed to think about that? You're here sitting with me, but you're with her."

"No, we're not," Nick said. "Not a chance."

"No?" She shook her head. "I don't believe you. You've orchestrated so much in my life in the last few months, so I don't know what to think."

Nick rested his elbows on his knees. "We had no idea what you've been through. Not recently. We knew your parents were in trouble and tried to help."

"We knew about your parents and were trying to shield you from the dangers involved with them. You're right. We'd tried to get help for your father, but it didn't work," Nathan said. "You weren't supposed to know because they didn't want to upset you."

"What?" She sagged in her seat. "Not tell me?" She should've guessed.

"Your father knew he was in trouble. He should've been in jail for selling heroin, but we managed to keep him out," Nick said. "He should've been on his way to jail shortly before the accident."

"So you knew about the accident?" She shot up from the couch and put space between her and the guys. "You'd talked to them? You know they used you. This was all a way to get your money and access for their own ends."

"We did." Nathan stood. "I assumed you knew about their passing. We didn't push anything that way, but we'd already made the decision to install you in our lives this way back then."

She needed a moment to absorb this information. They'd already had their eye on her? Her? It wasn't possible. "You should've told me—just like you should've told me you've been orchestrating my life. Getting me hired, helping my folks, watching me. You knew everything and you made me feel like it was all coincidence."

"We were wrong to intervene, but we were entranced by you." Nick joined them and stuffed his hands into his pockets. "We thought we were protecting you. We also thought you knew about their passing and now see the ball was dropped. We weren't kind, despite our best intentions."

"Well, now you know." She blinked back fresh tears. She'd been steeling herself for this day. With her parents' problems with drugs, any day could've been their last. She'd prepped herself, but that didn't take the sting away. Hell, she was numb. It was too much to deal with, and now she had her lovers dumping her to add to the emotional mix. "But I'll quit. You've done enough for me and it's time I leave the firm."

"No one says you're leaving." Nick reached for her.

"No." She shrugged away from him. "I'm not falling for that."

"Then fall for us." Nathan grasped her hand. "No one wants to leave you. We fucked up, but we tried. We fell in love with you. Yes, we were wrong to manipulate. We were so wrong, but that doesn't mean we weren't trying. No one is engaged — not to Suzy. We're happy with you. More than happy. Fuck, we're over the God damn moon. You leaving last night showed us just how much we screwed this up and how much we couldn't handle losing you."

"You can't?" She wanted to pull away, but didn't. Her escape opened their eyes? She'd finally done something right. "Why are you doing this to me? You were tangled up with her. I saw it."

"You did." Nathan slid his arm around her. "Listen to Nick. It's not what you think, and I've never wanted anyone else but you. Please believe us. Listen to him and let him explain."

She fought the urge to argue, barely holding on. "Then what happened?" she whispered. She wasn't ready for the information. Probably never would be.

"First, you're ours. We didn't invite you into our world to push you away. We invited you here because you're the one we want. My thoughts haven't been far from you all day." Nick tucked her to his side. "It's hard to think about meetings when I'd rather be at the penthouse kissing every inch of your body. I'd rather be nibbling the soft skin of your inner thigh and tasting that sweet pussy, rather than dealing with clients. Rather watching you walk away and knowing it's because we were too fucking thick to see what we'd done."

Some of her frustration evaporated. He might not be the perfect man, but he knew what to say to disarm her. Knew what to say to get her to believe him—like a lawyer should. But this felt different. It felt honest. Sweet. From the heart.

"Then what about Suzy?" She didn't pull away from Nathan, but forced her glare on Nick. "What about that production?"

"It was all hers." Nick sat on the arm of the sofa. "We figured out who'd breached the security system for the firm."

"Who?" She had no idea.

"Gert." Nick tipped his head. "She'd been giving Suzy information and going around our directives with the staff. If she wanted something, she got it. Suzy had given her money, so she used her information to get Suzy in. It's not been a good situation. When Suzy found out we'd settled down with you, she was livid. She used Gert's greed to get her into the building. Gert's been saying things all along about us hooking back up with Suzy—because she was being paid to say that."

"Meaning?" she asked. She couldn't process everything so fast. Gert hadn't struck her as a bad person, but more like demanding and gruff.

"Meaning those photos were staged," Nick said. "It was a complete coincidence that we fired Gert right before Suzy showed up. Suzy thought she had Gert on her side to get her in. The ring might have been real, but it wasn't from us. We'd never given her that kind of jewelry. But she thought we'd take her back and she had leverage. She waited until she knew we'd be seen and she forced the situation. The tabloids were paying attention and she played it for all she could."

She gritted her teeth. "Do you love her?"

"No, sweetheart." Nathan kissed her temple. "Never really did."

"We love you, darling." Nick crossed the expanse and added himself to the embrace. "When we saw you at the club, we were taken with you. We started the process to involve you in our life. Then we started the relationship with you and it solidified our feelings. We knew, in that moment, you were always supposed to be ours and we belonged to you."

"The scenes just proved how magnetic you are and how much we can't let you go." Nathan held her. "Come home. Please? Be ours and come home. We can't do this without you."

"You don't need me." She wasn't bending quite so easily.

"Want to bet?" Nathan rummaged in his pocket. "We bought this for you and had planned to give it to you tonight on our outing, but it can't wait." He held up a flocked box.

Too big for an engagement ring, not that she wanted one right now. She met his gaze, but didn't touch the box. "What is it?" she whispered. "I don't deserve it."

"You do." He opened the box, revealing a diamond necklace.

She gasped. The white stones sparkled against the deep blue velvet. The largest diamond was surrounded by smaller ones, forming an O. "It's beautiful."

"It's yours." Nick plucked the necklace from the box, then opened the clasp. "But this is a special piece. It's not something to be worn lightly." He arranged the necklace around her throat.

Nathan caressed her side. "This is our way of showing you that you belong to us. Heart, soul and body. Once we fix the clasp together, it's not coming off."

"No?" She switched her gaze between them. "Why not?"

"The clasp is a lock." Nick hesitated. "From this day forward, we vow to love, honor and cherish you. To give you pleasure beyond your wildest dreams, to make you fly, to push you, punish you, but always with love and respect. Our girl, our focus in the bedroom and our lover for the duration. Ours."

"You've got our heart and body. You're our third," Nathan said. "We have plenty of time to explore and stretch this relationship. Time to make it into what we desire. To be the triad we all deserve. Do you accept the necklace?"

She couldn't believe it. They were offering everything she ever wanted. All she had to do was take the chance.

"What do you think, Darinda?" Nick asked. "Will you?"

She didn't have to consider this much longer. "I will. I love you both." She kissed Nick, then Nathan. "I'd love to have your necklace and your vow. You've got mine."

"Good." Nick secured the necklace around her throat. "It suits you."

"Does it?" She swore her spirits were in the clouds.

"It does." Nathan kissed her temple. "Our girl."

"What about her?" She sobered a moment. "Will she come back into your life? Make trouble?" She wasn't sure she wanted to deal with Suzy again.

"No." Nick sighed. "The restraining order is in the works for Gert and already there for Suzy. The staff now knows not to let her onto the property, so there shouldn't be a problem."

"Good." That information relieved her. "I need a break."

"You do." Nathan guided her back to the sofa. "Have a seat, but come home with us. Please?"

"We were supposed to go out tonight, but you need time to relax." Nick sat beside her. "Movie and chill at the penthouse?"

Nathan settled on her other side. "With two men determined to make you happy? To do whatever you want to relax and recharge tonight?"

She laughed, knowing her life was still a mess, but she had the best partners to help her get it sorted out. "That would be fantastic."

"We love you, Darinda. You're ours." Nick curled his fingers under her chin and kissed her. "All the way."

"I second that," Nathan said and palmed her knee. "All the way ours."

She relaxed into them, knowing she'd found where she belonged. "And here I thought you didn't like me that much."

"Nah. We like you a whole lot more than a little," Nick replied.

"So much more." Nathan nuzzled her throat and palmed her upper thigh.

She had no doubt they'd make her the luckiest, happiest girl for the rest of her life. No doubts at all.

Chapter Fifteen

Nick grasped Darinda's hand. He'd been waiting for this night with her for so long. He'd known since the moment he'd met her that she was the one for them. Being with her before, all those times, had been wonderful, but tonight she'd fully be theirs. Time to head to the penthouse—her home. She belonged, not only in their house, but their lives forever.

"Grab your bag." Nick caressed her knuckles. "We'll have everything else moved to the penthouse as soon as possible."

She tensed just a bit. "Nick."

"It's not about taking control. We want you with us," Nathan said. "Losing you, even for the night, showed us how pushy we'd been and how we don't want you to go. It took a long time to find our third, so now we don't want this to end."

"It won't." She sighed and leaned into Nick. "I'm overwhelmed."

"I'm sure you are." Nick kissed the back of her hand. He wanted to take every one of her worries away. He and his brother would not only take care of her, but she'd be cherished. "If you let us, we'll be the men you need and want."

"You already are." She let go of him long enough to pack her shoulder bag.

Nathan fiddled with his phone, then stood by the door.

Impatient? Nick stared at Nathan until he finally met his brother's gaze. He tipped his head, in a silent question—what was Nathan doing? She should have their full attention.

Nathan held up his phone, showing the texting screen. Nick stared for another minute, finally able to make out some of the words. Nathan had summoned the car back around. *Good.* He nodded once more to his brother, then turned his attention to Darinda.

"Got everything?" Nick asked. He slid his hand along her back. "Sweetheart?"

"I do." She handed him the bag. "It's hard to give up my freedom, but I'll do it."

"You're not giving up anything. We're giving you more than freedom. You've got the chance to fly, to have whatever you want and two men who are completely, totally and wholly in love with you." Nick dropped the bag and cupped her jaw in both hands. "You're the rarest gem. A sweet woman with a heart of gold who has our hearts. You might be our sub, but you're everything to us and the one person we can't lose."

She leaned into him and whimpered. "I love you, too."

Nathan settled behind her, pinning her in between them. "Everything he's said is exactly how I feel, too."

"You're both too much to handle, but I can't imagine not being right here," she said. "With you."

"Then that's where you're going to stay." Nathan let go and picked up the bag. "Come on."

Nick guided her out of the apartment. He'd seen tired places. Living areas that needed more than a little TLC. She'd made her home light and filled with her personal touches, but still, she deserved more.

Once they were downstairs, Nick spotted the car. He directed her and Nathan to the vehicle. The splash of media wasn't around. Good. He wasn't in the mood to share this moment with anyone else. He ushered her and Nathan into the car. When he glanced over his shoulder, he spotted one lone cameraman. *Fine.* He smiled and winked behind his sunglasses, then joined his brother and their partner. As they sped away, he sighed. He'd dodged the media and could have precious hours with the woman he loved.

"You're pretty good at getting exactly what you want," she said. "I was very certain I wasn't interested. I loved you both, but I didn't want that life because I still don't think I belong here. I'm simple."

"You're not complicated, but you're unique. Who you are and what you've been through makes you the woman we chose. It's shaped you." Nick toyed with a lock of her hair. "Made you everything we love."

"I second that." Nathan massaged her thigh. "Makes me want you even more right now."

"If the ride across town was longer, I'd show my appreciation." She shifted her gaze between them. Fire lit her eyes. "Maybe I can when we get home."

"You will." Nathan nibbled on her neck. "And we'll show you the same."

Nick admired the view of his brother and their girl together. She looked so adorable between them. And so fully theirs. By the time the car reached the apartment, Nick swore he'd combust. He needed to have her upstairs and naked in their bed.

Nathan leaned back and sighed. "Home, kids." He left the car first, then held the door for her.

"Thank you." She hurried out to the corridor, then huddled against him. "Guys?"

"Yes?" Nick joined them and hurried to the penthouse with them just in front of him. "What's wrong?"

"I'm still in my pajamas," she said. "I never bothered to put on shoes."

"Then we need to do something about that." Nathan scooped her into his arms. He carried her to the bedroom.

Nick followed them and once Nathan set her on her feet, he and Nathan removed her clothing piece by piece. Her skin prickled and nipples beaded under Nick's gaze and he longed to kiss every inch of her.

Not yet.

Nathan nodded to Nick. "Ready?"

"I am." He focused on Darinda. "Are you ready?" He checked to ensure the necklace was permanently around her throat. The moment he looked into her eyes, a piece of him melted. He kissed her. The softness of her lips, the sigh vibrating in her and the way she arched into him pleased Nick. He tugged her to the bed and settled on the mattress. She crawled onto his lap, straddling him. He slid his palms over her naked breasts. Her nipples pebbled under his fingers.

"I love this." Nathan stroked her shoulders. "I need in."

His brother was there and he and Nathan knew how to work in tandem, but he wasn't interested in what his brother was doing. All that mattered was Darinda. He loved her body. Loved the curves and dips of her chest, the way she grinded on him, the moans and how she responded.

"You're gorgeous," he murmured, between kisses. "I love you."

She froze. Her mouth formed an O and she stared at him. "Nick?"

"I love you, too," Nathan said and resumed kissing her shoulder. "Ours."

"You are ours." Nick curled his fingers under her chin. "I know you're not ready to hear that on a regular basis, but it's true. This bauble is the symbol of our love on you forever."

"And that I belong to you. I won't get tired of hearing that we're three. That you love me." She draped her arms around his shoulders. "I'm ready to submit."

He memorized every last bit of her. The scent of her flowery perfume, the silkiness of her skin, the vibrancy in her eyes, the blush on her cheeks… Blood rushed to his cock and his nerve endings sizzled. He palmed her breast again and pinched her nipple hard. "Stand."

"Yes, sir." She slid off his lap and stood nude before him.

"My God." Nathan unbuttoned his shirt. "I can't wait much longer. We're going to use the paddle on you, clips, cuffs, a flogger…use you. Please you."

"I can't wait." She blushed all over. "Please? I need you."

He needed her as well. "Help me, girl." He scooted to the edge of the bed.

"Yes, sir." She knelt before him and popped the buttons on his shirt, then pushed his jacket off his shoulders. She unknotted his tie before sliding the silk from his collar. She gathered his jacket from the bed, and once he shrugged out of his shirt, she placed the garment on the chair with the jacket.

"Good girl." He kicked out of his shoes. "On your knees."

She did as she was told, settling on the floor. She rested her hands on her lap and bowed her head. "Ready, sir."

"Good girl." Nick rounded her, taking in the view of his precious gift. She was better than anything he could ever have imagined. "I think our girl needs some extra bling."

"She does." Nathan sat next to him on the bed. "Quite a bit." He produced a set of clips from his pocket.

Nick liked the choice. The little bells on the ends of the chain connected to each clip made a sparkling sound. Every time she moved, they'd know where she was. "Do you like these?"

Darinda nodded, but didn't look up. "Thank you, sirs."

"Stick out your chest." Nick palmed her breast, then plucked at her nipple before affixing the clip around the tender flesh. The silver metal glittered against her skin. With each breath, the bell jingled. "Beautiful."

"I second that." Nathan clipped the other binding to her free nipple.

A sense of calm swept over her face. The necklace caught the light and reminded Nick that he and his brother had made the right decision. She was truly theirs and would be forever.

Nick stood. "Open his pants."

"Yes, sir." Darinda worked free the zipper on Nathan's trousers, then freed his cock from behind his silk boxers and the expensive fabric.

"Show him you appreciate him." Nick selected a pair of cuffs from the drawer, then a paddle from the wall. The silicone of the paddle would create a loud noise and leave a mark, but wouldn't inflict much pain. He didn't want to hurt her, just get her attention.

Darinda didn't speak. Instead, she clasped her hands behind her back and buried her nose in Nathan's curls. She bobbed her head, taking Nathan deep before nearly pulling out.

The sight pleased Nick. He popped the spring on the cuffs. "Our girl needs this pretty, too." He secured the cuffs around her wrists, binding her. Darinda didn't stop blowing Nathan. Instead, she moved faster. A blush spread across her skin, giving her a glow.

Nathan threaded his fingers into her hair. "Fuck." He groaned and scooted down in his seat. He spread his legs, giving her better access. "Love it."

"I do, too." Nick grasped her hips, tugging her to her feet, while keeping her bent over Nathan. "Don't you dare stop."

She didn't. Nathan continued to guide her and she bobbed her head with abandon.

Nick shoved his pants and boxers to the floor. His cock glistened with pre-cum and he swatted the crack of her ass with the blunt head. "Want me inside you?"

She said nothing and continued to give attention to Nathan.

"Girl?" He swatted her hard with the paddle. A bright red mark appeared on her ass cheek. "Want another?"

She ripped her mouth away. "Yes, sir. More, sir. Please?"

Nathan guided her back to his dick. "Good girl."

Very good. He spanked her twice more, making the sound echo in the room. The more he spanked her, the more he wanted to be inside her. He added another swat, evening out the blows. Time to make her his. He tossed the paddle onto the bed and grasped her hips. Her pussy gleamed as he positioned her. She moaned.

God, he loved that sound. He pushed into her in one smooth thrust. The second he filled her, felt every ripple and nuance of her body, he knew he'd come home. He swatted her hip with his bare hand. "Mine."

"Ours." Nathan groaned. "Love this."

The cuffs jingled in time with the bells on her nipples. The sounds of her pleasure, her moans and whimpers, filled the air.

Nick would never get tired of this. Never want anyone else. He moved in perfect time with her and his brother, one soul, one body together. They'd found their person. He dug his nails into her hips. "Fuck." The pure desire of being with her rushed through his system. He loved having control, but ultimately, she had the power.

Just the thought she'd leave them freaked him out. He pistoned into her, losing himself in the thrill of fucking her. No, this was making love. It was a scene and so much more. She made him whole.

"I can't think." Nathan groaned. "Want to be inside her."

"Yeah?"

Nick growled. He'd been close to the edge before, but when she squeezed around him, she pushed him right over. He slammed into her, holding her tight to his groin. No way he'd ever let her go. His head swam. "Fuck." He'd come too fast, but he didn't care. As long as he was with her, then time didn't matter.

Darinda shivered. She wrenched her mouth free from Nathan another moment. "My knees are weak."

He'd just bet. Nick pulled out and kicked out of his wadded-up clothing. *Fuck it.* He didn't need them. "On his lap. Fuck Nathan. Show him how much you love being with us."

She glanced over her shoulder. "Yes, sir." She crawled onto Nathan's lap. "Hi."

Nick grinned. Other than having her in his own arms or between them in bed, this was the sweetest thing he could imagine. He never wanted anything else.

Nathan guided her onto his cock. He loved having her blow him, but he needed to feel her around him. The bells jingled as he bounced her and passion burned in her eyes. "Come for me," he whispered. "Let go."

She sighed and a soft grin spread across her lips. She writhed and grinded on him, forcing him deeper into her body. Her breasts jiggled with each movement, sending the music of the bells through the room.

Her head lolled on her shoulders. "More."

He held on to her, guiding each movement. He'd never be the same. Not now. She knew how to make him weak in the knees, hard as a rock and crave to protect her. No one else would do.

Nick stood behind her. He brandished the flogger, toying with the tails. "Make him moan."

She snapped her eyes open and met Nathan's gaze. "Yes, sir." As she continued to grind, she leaned forward and nibbled on Nathan's throat.

"Baby girl." He bounced her faster. She'd used her tongue so well on him, but having her pussy surrounding him was even better. He nodded to his brother, knowing what Nick had in mind.

Nick brought the tails of the flogger down on her shoulders. The move made her yip. She met Nathan's gaze again and a surge of heat shot from her body to his. She shivered.

"Good girl." He petted her hair. "Let go."

She nodded and her lips formed an O again. Nick peppered her back and shoulders with more blows from the flogger. The sound carried in the room, but Nathan didn't hear it. He trusted his brother. More, though, he needed to focus on her. The pleasure and desire on her face, in her eyes, spurred him on. He bounced her faster, pushing deeper into her. Each time he plunged into her body, he moved closer to orgasm.

Her movements turned feral and she squirmed. "I can't hold back."

"No?" Nathan threaded his fingers into her hair again and pulled her close. "Then come with me." He kissed her, sending himself over the edge. Nothing else mattered. The world melted away and his cares evaporated. All he saw was her.

Darinda shivered again and squeezed around his cock. She yelped into the kiss before sagging on him. Nick added a couple more swats from the flogger, before tucking the item under his arm.

Darinda panted. "I can't breathe."

"Then you've been sated." He surged into her once more, coming hard. He and his brother had found their girl. The collar she wore told the world she belonged to them and soon, he and Nick would have their showpiece to demonstrate to the world they belonged to her.

Nick stood behind her and unlocked the cuffs. "Curl on his lap. We'll hold you."

Darinda scooted off Nathan's dick, then tucked into herself on his thighs. She rested her head on his shoulder. While Nathan held on to her with one arm, he removed the clips. "Your poor sweet nipples."

"I loved it." She toyed with the day's whiskers on his chin. "The pain is the best."

"Yeah?" He cuddled her as she came down from the high. When Nick settled beside them on the couch, Nick palmed her hip.

"Not too rough?" Nick asked. "Talk to us."

"I feel fine," she said. "Better than fine. I'm at peace." She met Nathan's gaze. "No more running, hiding, no more feeling ashamed."

"Of what?" Nathan didn't want to hear her say such things. "What would you be ashamed of?"

Her eyes widened. "My family. My past."

"Those are chapters in the story of your life, but they aren't everything that makes up you." He toyed with her bottom lip. "Never doubt you're important to us. You're everything."

"I am?"

"Everything," Nick replied. "Until you, we weren't sure we wanted to settle down, wanted to marry, or even have life partners. Being single, playing the field and becoming grumpy old men wasn't a bad gig."

She snorted. "You're not grumpy."

"Ask our secretaries. We're grumpy," Nick said.

Nathan laughed. He'd always considered himself the pricklier of the two and more serious. To hear her say otherwise pleased him. She saw the true men, not the polished, cold veneer. "Then say you'll marry Nick and be our third."

"I'm already committed to you." She touched the necklace. "Don't need to be married. I know how I feel."

"You do?" Nick left the couch and returned a moment later donning his boxer shorts, but also holding the piece of paper. "We sketched something for you."

"Art, jewelry and declarations of love? I can't ask for more." She sat up on Nathan's lap. "I've got the best men in the world. I don't need anything else."

"You might want to look at this." Nathan caressed her back. "We're getting that ink — Nathan and I. Right here." He gestured to his outer wrist.

She frowned, then a smile curled on her lips. "That's your initials. Classy."

"No, sweetheart. Yours is in there, too. N, D, N. The three of us. A family, unit, partnership. Permanent." Nathan nodded. "Never letting you go. It took too long to find you. Now we can't imagine life without you."

She stared at him for a pregnant moment before a tear slipped down her cheek. "Just promise me you'll never take that back."

"Consider it a promise. Won't break it, ever." Nick grasped her hand. "Ours."

"Ours." Nathan sighed. He'd waited so long to find her and now that he had her, life was perfect. "You're the best arm candy we've ever had. So good, we're not relinquishing you."

"Arm candy?" She laughed. "That's all I am?"

"That's an honor. You're not just another pretty face." Nick shrugged. "Our girl sounds good to me."

Nathan caressed her cheek. "What do you want to be?"

"Yours," she replied. "But arm candy works, too. Glittery, sweet, eye-catching."

"And all ours—the girl with more than just a pretty face." He kissed her. The search was over and he'd never have to worry about his love life. He had the pieces in place to make it last forever. As long as he and Nick had Darinda, everything else would be just fine.

Chapter Sixteen

Darinda woke first the next morning. As she stretched, she shifted her gaze between her men. Nathan was so pretty in sleep and Nick looked tense. She slid her hands over Nick's belly and Nathan's hip. Touching them pleased her so much. They were her men.

Not anyone else's. Hers.

All she had to do was say their names and she'd have their full attention.

She wrestled free from the blanket, then scooted off the bed, trying not to disturb Nick or Nathan. They'd had a long evening and needed their sleep.

Then again, so had she. She'd stressed so much that they'd abandoned her.

Darinda inched over to the closet and selected one of the shirts from the hangers, then slipped her arms through the sleeves. She padded out of the bedroom to the living room and the bank of windows. The sunshine stretched across the city. She sighed. For once, she finally had the things she always wanted — a home, two men who loved her and she belonged.

Her phone beeped and she nearly jumped out of her skin. She rushed across the room to silence the device before she woke up her men.

She swiped to unlock the screen. A slew of text messages lit up as she tapped the icons. *What in the...* She wasn't even sure she knew that many people to text that much. The button lit up. Forty-seven messages.

Good Lord. She retrieved the messages and her heart nearly stopped. Gavin had messaged her twice, but the rest were from three numbers she didn't know. She swiped through the texts, but as soon as she panicked, she relaxed. The numbers might have been unknown to her, but the second she saw the contents of the texts, she knew what was going on.

One number simply texted links. She refused to tap any of them and deleted them all. The second number had messages, but every one of them accused her of stealing Nick. She hadn't stolen anyone. Had Suzy gotten her number? Most likely, but she didn't care.

Darinda blocked the second number and deleted the texts. The third number's messages practically mirrored the ones coming from the one she presumed to be Suzy.

"Block," she murmured and did just that — blocked the number and deleted the messages.

She switched to the messages from Gavin.

Hey girl. Saw you've accepted the challenge. Good luck to you. I'm glad. You're adorable together.

She couldn't help, but beam. Gavin approved and that made her happy. She didn't need his okay, but she liked having it. Gavin had a keen sense and she should've listened to him sooner.

She checked the second message.

By the way, I got the gig at Sixxes for two years. Thank you. Couldn't have done it without you.

He'd gotten what he wanted, too. She tapped to call him, not bothering to check the hour of the day. Five rings, then he answered.

"Do you know what time of day it is?" Gavin asked.

"No, but I couldn't wait." She sank onto the couch. "Two years! It's what you've always wanted."

"I've wanted it since we first started attending Sixxes," Gavin said. "It's an honor. I guess they saw how I handled you, how I worked with the other Doms and I was given the chance to show my skills with other subs. I haven't chosen a sub and I'm not sure if I will, but there's time."

"You have to pick one?"

"It was suggested I do it for the short term. That way I can do demonstrations with the same sub. It's a matter of safety, continuity and smarts. Safe because it's the same person and we trust each other, continuity because it's the same sub and we can make it look seamless, but also smarts, because we can play at any time and it looks authentic."

"Wow." She hadn't realized there was so much to consider.

"But enough about me. You knew I'd get the job because I wasn't going to stop until I did," Gavin said. "What about you? I saw your photos all over the internet. You're famous for being the one the famous Reid brothers chose. I bet you had no idea."

"I didn't." She wanted to look herself up, but didn't. If the photos were from yesterday, then people would've seen her leaving the apartment in her long T-shirt, no shoes and bare legs. Fuck, she hadn't even been wearing a bra. She probably looked like a hot mess.

"Hey, you're a princess." Gavin laughed. "It's crazy, but I'm proud of you. I wasn't sure you'd make the decision to give them another chance."

"I almost didn't."

"Why not? Sweets, you love them."

"I do."

"Then what?"

She sighed. "I had a long conversation with someone I trust and he set me straight. He gave me some good advice about giving it some time."

"He sounds pretty smart."

"He is."

"Separation helped?"

"Sort of," she replied. "I got stuck in my head. I mean, you know my situation. I wasn't exactly princess material. If my mother, God rest her soul, knew I'd been such a hot mess club kid, she'd have killed me."

"Stop. Your mother was a colossal mess and would've wanted to be at the clubs with you. She'd have been making plays for the brothers."

She pinched the bridge of her nose. "Probably."

"You do realize it doesn't matter where you came from, what you did in the past or how much of a mess you might have looked like at whatever point. Those guys are over the moon for you because you're a doll. They're lucky to have you."

"I'm lucky to have them. They've made me feel like I'm more than I am."

"You always were," he replied. "You're a diamond that got lost in the dust, but has now been found and you've polished yourself. Don't forget that."

"I won't." She still wasn't ready to accept it, but she'd follow his advice. "When do you go back to Sixxes and work?"

"I'm on the books to be there tomorrow," he said. "Are you still fired?"

She paused. *Well, fuck.* "I don't know." She hadn't asked and they hadn't said. "It hasn't been discussed. I suppose I don't."

"Do you really want to work for them?"

She had to think about that, too. "Honestly?"

"Honestly."

"I would rather work. I'd like the chance to have something of my own. I get that they want to provide for me and I'm not ignoring it, but I've been independent. I don't mind being kept, but I'd like to have something that's mine. Something I can do."

"You should," Gavin said. "You did a damn good job building yourself up."

"Thanks." She hadn't thought he'd noticed. When she looked up, she noticed Nathan in the doorway. She hadn't done anything wrong, but she wondered if she should end the call.

"Hey, I've got to go. I need sleep so I'm awake enough to head to the gym later. Don't be a stranger and don't forget me when you're famous-er," Gavin said. "Sex them up and make me proud."

"I will. See you." She hung up, then left the phone on her lap. "Hi."

Nathan remained in the doorway. "Hi."

She wanted to curl into herself. "I bet you heard all of that."

"I did."

"And?" She winced. He might not want her to have a job. Might not be thrilled she'd talked to her friend. "Wait. Before the lecture, I need to say this."

"You've got the floor." He tipped his head, but stayed in the doorway.

"I was speaking to my friend Gavin. If you and Nick watched me as much as I think you did, then you saw me with him. He's a friend, but I've done scenes with him because he was trying to get a spot at Sixxes. He's smart, funny and not at all interested in me, but he's a good friend. He's the reason I'd planned to call you yesterday, but you both showed up before I could."

"What'd he say?" Nathan finally wandered across the room and sat opposite her on the sofa. "Something worthy, I assume."

"He told me to wait. Give it—us—a day or two to cool down, then talk. I wasn't going to wait much longer." She picked at the hem of the shirt. "He also told me you and Nick were just nuts about me. About as nuts as I am about you. He said you both watched me when we played and that shit about Suzy was just that—shit. He told me to trust you."

"And today?"

"He'd texted that he'd earned the position with Sixxes, so I wanted to congratulate him. He worked hard to get that slot, so it's worth the call."

"I'm sure it is."

His odd sentences and calm demeanor confused her. "He also asked how I was feeling. If I'd called you or at least had a sit down." After she spoke, she wished she could edit her words. "I mean…did we hash it out. I told him we had and that I was here."

"You did." He watched her and a slight smile formed on his lips. "But you also mentioned a job. Being independent. Or did I hear you wrong?"

"No." There wasn't any point in lying. "I did."

"Okay? What did you decide?"

"What do you mean?"

"You said you wanted a job."

"I do."

"You have one."

"Being in your bed?" She sighed. "I want more than that. More out of life."

"Who said you won't have more?"

He'd confused her again. "Nathan."

"I never said you were fired. I believe Nick and I determined you weren't," he said. "What your specific job will be hasn't been determined, but that doesn't mean you don't have one. You made a valid point. You want some independence. You want to be your own person. A job will give you that. Besides, we don't want to hold you down that way. Sweetheart, we want you to fly. If that's working and being your own person, then do it. We fell in love with you because you are your own person."

She stared at him, needing a few moments to process what he'd said. She knew what he'd said, but the words had to wash over her. They didn't mind her being herself. *Holy shit.*

"I thought about us having a discussion concerning your place at the firm. I don't want you to be our personal assistant, but if you want a job, then you should have one. I'd like to have you close so we can have trysts. I mean, I'd like our partner to be available. I'd also like you to be permanently naked on the sofa in my office."

His words touched her. "Nathan." She scooted over to him. "You're too good to me."

"I'm good to you because you deserve it." He gathered her on his lap. "I don't get gooey about many people. Ask Nick. He likes to tease me that I'm cold as ice, especially in the courtroom."

"When's the last time you were in court?" She hadn't known him to go.

"That's the beauty of being the heads of the firm. Nick and I don't have to go if we don't want to. We simply let everyone else handle the caseload and simply practice enough to stay current. We've done our time in court and now it's time for others to do that." He patted her ass. "By the way, you make my shirt look damn fine."

"I wasn't sure if it was yours or Nick's, but it was a pretty shade of yellow and soft."

"It looks good on you." He curled his fingers under her chin. "I want to part the front, caress your breasts and play with your sweet little nipples."

"Who says you can't?" She shrugged out of the shirt, letting it fall around her elbows. The cool air swirled around her and her nipples hardened. Heat filled her belly and she sighed. He made her feel alive and sexy. Wanted. She longed to give him the same pleasure he and Nick gave her.

"No one." He slid his hands around her waist and toyed with her navel. "You're gorgeous."

"I'm just me." She rested her hand on his wrist.

"You being you is fine."

"I never feel like I'm ever enough." She shifted on his lap, grinding on his burgeoning erection. "It's terrible."

"It is, but we'll help you work on your confidence." He scooped her into his arms and left the sofa. He carried her across the room. As he moved, the shirt landed on the floor.

She wanted to retrieve the garment, but didn't bother. Being in his embrace was more intoxicating. She kissed him, loving every second. When he groaned, she nibbled along his jaw to his throat, then back up to his cheek to his lips. He opened to her, sucking on her tongue. He placed her on the bed, then let go and shoved his boxers to the floor.

She ogled his naked body. Every curve, dip and sinew enticed her. She reached for him. "Come here."

Nick rolled over and slid his arm around her. "What are you doing?"

"I'm about to make love to Nathan." She allowed Nick to turn her toward him. "Or should I make love to you?"

"Both," he said. "Right now."

The predatory tone of his voice spurred her on. She parted her legs, allowing him to touch her wherever he wanted. As he slid his fingers along her pussy, she cried out. He speared one finger into her cunt. "Nick."

"Suck him," Nathan said. "Show me your pretty ass."

She loved being pushed this way. It wasn't a specific scene, but she didn't care. Their love and attraction, plus devotion was enough. She grinded on Nick's finger a bit more, then shifted position and pushed the bedding aside. His cock bobbed before her. Pre-cum glittered on the tip.

She licked her lips before easing down onto his shaft. He filled her mouth and the taste of him exploded on her tongue. He slid his hand along the back of her head, not pushing, but guiding and allowing her to set the pace. She curled her tongue around his shaft, then glanced up at him. The passion in his eyes added to the intensity of the moment.

Nick toyed with her hair and wound some of the strands around his fingers. He pulled slightly and the pain added to her pleasure.

She bobbed her head, taking him to the back of her throat before nearly pulling out. Each time she surged down onto him she wanted to cry out. His murmurs filled the room. He pulled again on her hair.

"Yes, babe. Do it. Fuck, I love it." Nick arched his back, meeting her actions with those of his own and slamming into her mouth.

She loved being pushed this way. She might have the tempo, but he held the control.

At the same time, Nathan caressed her bare ass. He ran his thumb along the crinkled skin of her hole. He managed to touch every sensitive nerve ending with each pass. He swatted her, pushing her down on Nick's cock.

She spread her legs, giving Nathan more access to her backside. She needed him to breach her. To push her. Something cool slid down the crease of her ass and she shivered, but continued to lap at Nick.

"Breathe, sweetheart." Nathan swatted her again, this time a bit harder. "Relax."

She tried, but the excitement of knowing he'd be inside her soon was too much. Every nerve ending tingled. The scent of their cologne curled around her and the spicy pre-cum tasted like heaven. She'd never be the same.

"Breathe," Nathan whispered. He added more lube, sending a fresh shiver through her, then pushing one digit into her ass. He eased past the tightness until he filled her to the hilt. She rocked back onto his finger then down onto Nick's cock in a delightful cadence.

"Good girl. Pulling me in," Nathan said. "So tight and perfect."

She liked the way he fucked her, too. She bobbed her head faster, riding the wave of pleasure. The tingles started low in her belly and spiraled through her body. She curled her toes and balled her hands in the blankets. A cry strangled in her throat. She swallowed Nick deep, burying her nose in his curls. She was their toy, their girl. A prize. She loved that.

Nathan pushed harder, then added more lube and a second finger. He scissored her, opening her. "Relax." He spanked her again. "Give in to the delicious feeling."

She didn't need his coaxing. She was already there. Being used this way blew her mind. She couldn't breathe or think. Not when he and Nathan consumed her thoughts. She loved the way they tasted, the pressure of their touch, the scent of them and the pleasure of being theirs. The sound of Nathan fucking her ass with his fingers made her heart sing. She let go long enough to drag a deep breath into her lungs. Her skin sizzled and the heat threatened to engulf her.

"Want to ride?" Nick asked. He trailed his fingers across her swollen lips. His eyes flashed. "Want to come apart?"

"Yes." On both accounts. She needed both men inside her and the biggest orgasm of her life.

"Climb on." Nick held out his hands. "Come here."

She glanced back at Nathan, who withdrew his hand. He nodded to her. She grinned. She wasn't sure what all they had in mind for her, but she'd be happy.

Invitation accepted.

Chapter Seventeen

Nathan popped the cap on the lube as he watched Darinda climb onto Nick's cock. She was beautiful when dressed, stunning when nude and a knockout while settling on Nick's dick. She straddled Nick's lap. Her skin blushed and her head lolled.

Nathan had never seen anything so captivating. He crawled onto the bed and planted his knees. He reached around her body and grasped her breast, rolling her nipple in his fingers. "Want me inside you, too?"

She glanced over her shoulder. "I do."

Her tone nearly turned his insides out.

Nick held on to her hips, rocking her forward and baring her ass. He kept thrusting into her, but slowed his pace long enough to allow Nathan the chance to fit himself in her hole.

Nathan lined himself up with her asshole and pushed. He drenched his dick with lube, sinking into her. The heat and desire in her enveloped him. Power like he'd never known surged through his body. She was theirs. Filling her like this, overtaking her and owning her, while having little control himself, made him fly.

Within a few seconds, he and his brother built into a steady rhythm, fucking her. When Nick surged in, Nathan withdrew. A few times, they both slammed into her at the same time.

She gasped and dug her fingers into Nick's shoulders. "Oh. Fuck." She curled into him. "Love it."

"Love you." Nathan lost himself in the sheer pleasure of being inside her. The rest of the world seemed to melt away. He had the piece he'd been looking for all his life because he had her. Everything else was just noise. She mattered. She made him whole.

Nick cried out. "Fucking balls. I need to come. Fuck."

Not the most eloquent thing he could've said, but Nathan understood. He was just as frazzled as his brother. "Come." He wanted to say more, but the words were gone. All he could do was experience the moment and ride the wave.

She shivered, then tensed. "I can't..." She trembled as she came. She clamped her ass around him, then went slack against Nick.

"Fuck." Nick surged into her and stilled. "My God."

Nathan wanted to laugh with sheer pleasure, but instead, he forced himself to focus on embracing his orgasm. He could be himself with Darinda. They could be the power triad he'd always imagined. They both embraced him for who he was. Everything else was just static.

The orgasm built low in his groin, then spiraled through his body to his limbs, then centered in his heart. His control splintered and he slammed into her.

He gave into the climax. As he filled her ass with his cum, his heart overflowed with love for her. He braced himself on his hands and knees, then added a few more thrusts before stilling.

Good God, his thoughts were a mess.

He sighed and eased his dick from her ass, sorry to have to be apart from her, then collapsed beside his brother on the bed.

Darinda seemed to melt into the slight space between Nick and Nathan. Nathan slid his arm around her. She fit so well — their missing piece. The glue holding everything together.

He said nothing and neither did Darinda or Nick. Just being together and listening to the sound of their heavy breathing was enough.

After what seemed like forever, but was probably only a few moments, Darinda finally spoke. "You blew my mind."

"Mine, too," Nick managed. "Felt good." He twined his legs with hers.

"Good?" Nathan laughed. "She was fucking fantastic." He dragged the sheet over their bodies. Not to cover them up, but to envelope them in the softest wrappings. To shield them from the rest of the world. To symbolize their union in body and soul.

"She was," Nick said. He curled against Darinda's side and cupped her breast in his hand. "Our kind of fantastic."

"She is." Nathan sighed. "We're not letting go." He knew that to the bottom of his heart.

"Not for one second." Nick's voice came out sleepily. Within seconds, he began to softly snore.

Darinda shrugged. "I did my job, didn't I?"

"You did." Nathan kissed her bare shoulder and held on to her. She'd done so much for them, but she'd also done a lot for him. She'd given him the chance to find his heart and believe that love could be his. She gave him hope.

For a man who believed he was beyond love or a future with the right partner, she'd shown him anything was possible. As long as he had Darinda, he could do anything.

He'd found the golden ticket in life — Darinda.

* * * *

Two months later…

Nick headed up to the penthouse. He'd put in too many hours hashing out an agreement over a housing situation. He hated haggling when he could simply put forth terms and have them accepted. But not everyone was as cooperative. People didn't seem to like his pushiness.

Oh well. He wasn't going to please everyone.

He kicked off his shoes, then strode across the lower level of the penthouse. He hadn't wanted to work today, but the client had insisted on getting the deal done. Who was he to argue? It meant good money, not that he needed it.

"Darinda?" He tossed his phone onto the counter. If the damn phone didn't ring for a while, he'd be happy. "Nate?" Where were they? He and Nathan had ensured Darinda had a job at the firm in human resources, aiding the interviews and helping to select prospective talent. She had a vital role for the firm. She understood the fears and worries by the people being interviewed and could talk to them. She had patience when he didn't.

Nathan strode down the steps. "You're back."

"I am. Where's Dar?" He unhooked his cufflinks before tossing them onto the counter with his phone.

"Contentious meeting?" Nathan padded barefoot across the living room. "Dar's upstairs talking to Gavin. He phoned earlier."

"Oh." He unbuttoned his shirt, then let the sleeves hang loose. "How's he doing?" The very idea that he and his brother were talking about another man in Darinda's life like it was nothing amazed him. His predatory nature and his desire to protect her were stronger than he'd ever imagined.

"They're just catching up." Nathan poured a glass of wine, then offered one to his brother. "He's happy at Sixxes and wondered if we'd come back."

Nick accepted the goblet. "Yanno, we just went there to find someone. It's a nice club, but I don't know that we need to return."

"I agree." Nathan sipped his drink. He leaned on the bar, then crossed his ankles. "I was thinking about our membership there. It's not like we need to return. Hell, we haven't been back since the night we watched her with Gavin. It's hot to see her so submissive, but I'd rather her be that way with us at home. She likes being shown off, but I don't want to. I want to parade her around here. For our eyes only."

"I'm not arguing." He swirled the wine in the glass and breathed in the soft bouquet. His brother always bought good wine and he didn't have to wonder if this one would be wonderful. He sipped the tart drink and let the taste slide over his tongue. Intoxicating — almost as wonderful as kissing Darinda.

"Good? It's a small batch." Nathan held on to his glass. He swirled the wine without drinking it. "We relinquish our membership?"

"We should." He drank a bit more then sighed. "And if we want to go back, we can. I'd imagine she'd want to be there every so often."

"She might." Nathan dipped his head.

"What's on the agenda for tonight?" He left his glass on the bar. "Are we doing anything?"

"Last I checked, no." Nathan finished his wine. "She said something about a movie and chill. Popcorn, snuggly pajamas and tangled up in the couch, I believe she said."

"I like that." He nodded and contemplated finishing his wine. He wanted to see her first. "The clients were angry we hadn't finished the agreement. I can't finish what's not ready to be done. It's nuts."

"It is." Nathan left the bar. "I had my will changed today. I left everything to you and Dar. Equal. I don't want something to happen and it be a disaster. You both deserve what's there."

He hadn't wanted to think about anyone dying, but it made sense. He should update his own will. "We can't marry her. Not both of us."

"I know." Nathan folded his arms and leaned on the bar again. "Which is why I changed the will. We can't both marry her, but we can ensure she's protected."

He agreed. "What if we have one of those symbolic weddings? Something where it's not legal, but it's a gesture. A sealing together?"

"We already collared her, so to speak."

"We did." But he wanted something more.

"We'll figure it out. We know we want her, she wants us and we're three. There's no question of that.

Whatever will happen will. It'll sort out," Nathan said. "She taught me not to think too hard about the future, but plan enough that everyone's okay."

"You're probably right." He drank the rest of his wine. "I need some Darinda. To curl up on the couch like she wants and just exist."

"I believe it was veg out." Nathan grinned and unfolded himself. He headed across the room to the steps. "She's got it all set upstairs."

"Then let's go." He'd do whatever she wanted. If he could keep her kisses coming, hold her all night and make love to her whenever he wanted, then he'd do what she wanted. Without question.

When he and his brother ascended the steps, Darinda was already stretched out on the sofa. She wore a simple T-shirt, her legs bare, white ankle socks, and held on to one of the pillows. She'd pulled her hair back in a ponytail and wore no makeup.

For a moment, she stole Nick's breath. The woman made beauty effortless. "Hi, sweetheart."

She brightened and sat up. "I wondered what took Nathan so long. How was your day?"

"Just another one." He crossed the room to her. Nathan sat on one side and he took up the other. He slid his hand over her bare thigh. "Doesn't matter what happened today. None of it matters because I'm home with the people I love the most."

She kissed Nathan, then kissed Nick. "I'm with the ones I love the most, too."

He settled in beside her. "So we're vegging out this evening?"

"I suggested it." She laughed. "Unless you have a better idea."

Nathan cleared his throat. "Honey, we always have better ideas, but we haven't had a night to relax, so I'm game for this."

"Nick?" She tipped her head. "What do you think?"

"I agree with Nathan, that there's always another idea, but this one will work. Besides, we don't have to simply watch the movie. If we happen to allow the movie to encourage other activities…"

"I like how you think." She massaged his crotch with one hand and massaged Nathan with the other. "I didn't tell you what movie we'd be watching."

"No, you didn't." Nathan groaned and shifted in his seat. "But whatever it is, I love it."

Nick drew in a long breath, then exhaled. He didn't give a shit what movie they'd be watching. As long as they ended up naked at the end, he'd be happy. "I'm in."

He wasn't sure if the movie ever started. All he saw was Darinda and all he wanted was to make her cry out. He'd found his heart when he'd seen her because she wasn't just another pretty face. She was their one.

Sign up for our newsletter and find out about all our romance book releases, eBook sales and promotions, sneak peeks and FREE romance books!

Want to see more from this author?
Here's a taster for you to enjoy!

Club Sixxes: Another Curvy Body
Wendi Zwaduk

Excerpt

I want to be with someone who could love me. Chloe Hunter waited in line at Tracks and patted her watch. When she clubbed, she insisted on wearing the timepiece because it contained her credit card information, her ID and the key to her car. No cards to lose, keys to misplace or purse to carry.

"You here for the dancing or the conversation?" a man behind her asked. He bumped her ass. "Or selling?"

She stepped backward, pretending to trip while intentionally jamming the spiked heel of her shoe into the top of his foot. She glanced back and pasted a ditzy smile on her face. "Sorry! These sidewalks are so uneven." She giggled. "I stepped wrong. Sorry."

"No problem." He winced. "If you're here to dance, then you'd better be careful."

"I try to." She kept up the dizzy blonde act. Guys tended to like the facade. She never had understood why. She wanted a partner who accepted her beauty *and* her brains.

"Are you meeting someone here?" he asked.

The heel to the foot wasn't going to get him to leave her alone? Interesting. She clasped her hands together and swept her gaze over him. Not her type at all. Blond men didn't do much for her. Plus, he wasn't much taller than her five-foot-three. She liked tall men. But he did have a boyish charm to him…almost a fake charm. She'd seen a hundred men like him — trying too hard to be either a tough guy or sweet to the point of disarming.

"I'm just here to dance. Not buying or selling or conversation." She shrugged, then turned her attention to the door as the line moved forward. She wished she wasn't to the point of wanting to be with anyone who could love her. She should be with someone who fell hard for her. Wanted her as much as his next breath.

Like that was going to happen.

"I'm meeting my girlfriend," the man offered. "She's here as a bottle girl."

"Oh good." She wasn't sure if this was a lie to make her jealous or showing off. She'd guess the latter. "See you later." She headed up to the bouncer and paid her fee, then went into the club.

The fool behind her, if he was indeed dating a bottle girl, had to know better than to ask if she was there for conversation. The music was too damn loud. Any conversation had to be made at the bar, shouting, or outside on the patio. Even the restrooms were full of pumped-in music.

The bass thumped and people were already jammed into the room. The first time she'd gone clubbing, someone had told her there'd be plenty of space and making connections with people would be easy.

Both were dead wrong.

She noticed the talker from the line dart over to one of the bottle girls and engage her in conversation.

Good luck. She turned her back on him and threaded her way into the crowd. The throb of the bass, the wave of the bodies and the sheer onslaught of sensations were too much. She let herself get caught up in the wave and danced. Nothing else mattered, just existing.

She didn't notice anyone or anything besides the music. The rollicking dance music made her happy. She could be anyone she wanted for a few hours in the club. If someone tried to talk to her, she'd pretend to be an heiress or a street kid. She could be anyone but Chloe, the girl who worked in a law office and had spent the last three years of her life balancing work and taking care of her father.

She wished Darinda had come out tonight to the clubs. At least she'd have someone to hang out with and not feel so alone. The last she knew, Darinda wasn't into the clubs — or hadn't been until she'd gotten tangled up with the Reid brothers. Lucky girl. Two insanely rich men who wanted nothing but her attention.

Like that would happen to her.

She danced a while longer, then pushed her way to the bar. She waved to the bartender and held up two fingers. The bartender nodded before opening a bottle of water for her.

She tapped her watch to pay for the water and leave a tip, then downed the drink in nearly two gulps. Dancing gave her release, but it also wore her out. She ducked over to the patio and finished the water.

Coming to the club wasn't going to change her life. It wasn't going to make anything better — except it did. She watched the crowd and wished she wasn't quite so shy. She could dance into the middle of the throng of bodies with no problem and make mild small talk, but letting someone in? That was the impossible part. Guys who came to Tracks weren't interested in a relationship. They wanted a hook-up.

She'd been the good-time girl a few times and it hadn't ever felt right. Why sleep with someone just to leave them the next morning and never see them again? Why put herself out there?

Because she'd never find someone otherwise.

Chloe tossed the bottle in the recycling can, then ducked into the middle of the dancers. She moved to the music again and lost herself in the chaos around her. Some people understood how to dance, but most had no idea. They simply moved. One man caught her attention because he appeared to be throwing elbows — not to hurt anyone. No, he seemed to have no sense of rhythm.

She turned and another man grabbed her attention. This one wasn't anywhere close, but the moment she saw him, she didn't want to look anywhere else.

He caught her gaze and smiled.

Something low in her belly turned to mush. Guys didn't usually have this effect on her. She could be cool and distanced. Yes, she might fall in lust with them, but it was always from afar. The instant gut reaction wasn't usual for her.

He sailed through the crowd to her. Although she couldn't understand a word he said because she couldn't hear him above the crowd, she allowed him to take her hand. She walked with him to the patio.

"God, it's loud in there." He let go and held the door for her.

"It is." She ducked under his arm, moving out to the patio. Unlike in the club, she could see the various bouncers outside. Inside, the club used a bank of cameras and a few big men for intervention. If this guy bothered her, she'd be protected.

"I saw you in line." He nodded to the bar. "Want a drink?"

"I'm good." She leaned on the fence and crossed her ankles. "You saw me, huh? Where in line?"

"By the door." He laced his fingers together as he leaned his elbow on the fence. "You were being annoyed by the guy behind you."

"You saw that?" She kept her expression blank, so she didn't give away too much interest. The more men thought she was interested, the harder they pushed. If he liked her, even a little bit, then he'd have to work for her affection.

"I did. I know him, too. He's pushy. Wants to hook up with anyone who shows attention." He chuckled. "Did he give you the story about the bottle girl?"

"He did." She eyed him. She'd never seen him at this club. Hadn't seen him anywhere. "You know him?"

"He's an installer. Puts in cabinets and countertops. Nice enough guy, but he's desperate to get laid." He nodded as the female bartender brought him a martini. "Thanks."

"How do you know all that?" She folded her arms. "You just know the backstories of people here?"

"Not exactly." He sipped the drink. "I don't know anything about the bartender. Never met her before."

"Oh." She sighed. "So the installer…what's his story? He's desperate for a date?"

"He's a nice guy, but he's not versed with the fairer sex and tries too hard. He came on to a friend of mine and didn't take it well when she turned him down."

"Friend?" Codeword, *girlfriend*. "I see."

"I doubt you do." He sipped more of the drink. "He's a friend and so is she, but I don't want to date her. Never have."

Another man joined them and her mouth watered. Where the man speaking to her was sexy, this one practically oozed sex appeal as well. Both exuded power. Tall, dark, handsome, soft spoken and not pushy. At least not yet.

She suppressed a shiver. "Hi."

"Hi." The second man crooked his brow. "I see you've met Justin. I'm Martin."

She accepted his hand when he stuck it out and shook hands with Martin. She hadn't gotten around to asking Justin his name. "It's nice to meet you, Martin. Justin has been entertaining me for the last few minutes." She turned her attention to Justin. "It's nice to meet you, too."

"Martin would've busted my balls, but I forget my manners and to introduce myself." He left his half-empty glass on the table in front of them. "Forgive me."

"You're forgiven." She snorted. She wasn't sure what he played at, but if he wanted her attention, he had it. "Why are you talking to me?"

"Huh?" Martin inclined his head. "Why wouldn't we?"

"I'm not out there shaking my ass all over everywhere, not letting my boobs hang out, not throwing myself at you. There are fifty others in there who'd do that." She had a tendency of talking herself out of things she deserved. "Sorry."

"You don't have to be sorry." Justin stood tall and hooked his fingers in his pockets. "You're right. There are others who would throw themselves our direction."

"But I'm not?" she asked.

"You're beautiful and caught my attention," Justin replied. "I wanted to talk to you. Get to know you."

"Is that bad?" Martin asked. "It's not like you can have a conversation in the club. Jesus, you can't hear a nuclear explosion in there."

An odd turn of phrase, but true. "Sorry."

"You've been hurt, haven't you?" Justin asked. "Been jerked around in there?"

She shrugged to disguise her frustration. So she had been jerked around, as they put it. So what? She'd been used a few times in there, too. She didn't feel like she belonged. But what was new?

"I'd take you to the VIP section, but it's not any quieter there. It's better out here," Martin said. "Would you like a drink?"

"No, thank you." She liked to keep her wits about her. "How about a dance?"

"Out here?" Martin's eyes flashed.

The predatory look did something for her. The twinge in her belly? No. The shiver up her spine? Not quite. Her pussy thrum? Yes. He made her wet with that glance. She turned her attention to Justin. He created the same reaction within her. She wanted to shimmy between them and feel both men touch her.

"Come on," she said and grasped each man's hand. "I like this song." She led them back into the main room of the club just beyond the edge of the dancers. The position gave her plenty of room to be with them, but also the opportunity to disappear if they got too grabby. She positioned herself between them.

Martin tucked in behind her, rubbing her ass along his groin. He slid his hands over her hips. He brushed his lips across her bare shoulder.

She bit back a groan and thanked God she'd decided to wear a strappy dress tonight. She loved when her partner kissed her shoulders and the back of her neck.

Justin fitted against her, chest to chest and groin to groin. He draped her arms around his neck. His smile warmed her to her core. She swayed with him and Martin as one body moving to the beat of the music. Justin nuzzled her jaw. His breath tickled her skin. She gazed into his eyes and her breath wrenched from her body. She loved men with brown eyes. When she stared into his eyes, so deep and dark she could get lost in them, she whimpered. She longed to straddle his thigh and ride him.

She moaned. Being between them, caged, but also protected, excited her. She loved the way they touched her. The tenderness and sweetness were more than she could handle. She tipped her head back and rested it against Martin's shoulder. When Justin palmed her breast, she cried out — not that anyone could hear her. She snapped her eyes open and parted her lips. He hadn't pinched or grabbed. A simple sensual caress. Her nipple beaded beneath his fingertips. She loved the instant reaction to him and the way he made fire surge through her veins. She gasped.

Justin let go and turned her around, allowing her to face Martin. He had the same dark eyes, but a few more lines around those eyes. Where Justin was almost baby-faced, Martin was a bit more weathered. He smiled and her knees weakened. She draped her arms around his neck and rubbed her nose along his. Part of her wanted to strip naked and give herself over to him.

To them.

Justin grinded behind her, but it wasn't lascivious. More like one of the most sensual things she'd ever done in her life. He moved with reverence. Touched her like she mattered.

Martin trailed his fingers along her arm, then kissed her. She'd imagined his lips would be soft, but she hadn't expected the connection to be that intoxicating. She opened to him immediately and sucked on his tongue. The man was like velvet. She groaned into the kiss. He threaded his fingers into her hair and held her close while Justin caressed her from behind.

She barely heard the music and the crowd was non-existent. Nothing else mattered except being between these two men. She danced and luxuriated in their attention. For once, she felt important, but also cherished and desired.

She broke the kiss and continued to dance with them. Martin swayed with her and grinned. His toothy smile hinted at a boyishness he probably hid. She wasn't sure what he might do for a living. His dress and demeanor didn't give away his profession.

Right now, she didn't care.

As she danced, she slid her hand over Justin's cheek. Touching him sent electrical sparks through her system. The same thing happened when she rubbed against Martin. She'd never been attracted to two men at once. She tended to be a one-man woman. But being between them made her rethink her choices.

Her wrist vibrated and she checked the message on her watch. A text. *Shit*.

Come home. Madelin ran away.

She groaned. Her sister Melinda didn't understand her own daughter, Madelin, and expected Madelin to simply go along with her mother's wishes. Chloe wasn't a parent, but she'd taken care of her father for the last three years until the cancer won. Some days she wasn't sure how she'd made it to twenty-eight with her wits intact. The one thing she did know was that the more Melinda pushed Madelin, the more Madelin separated from the family. She also knew what'd happened to Madelin, though. The young woman had run away and most likely, Chloe knew where she'd gone.

She disengaged from both men and wished she didn't have to leave.

Before she got too far, Martin grasped her fingers. He tipped his head. She pointed to the patio.

Justin and Martin followed her to the relatively quiet space of the patio.

"I need to go," she said. "Long story short, my niece ran away and she's probably at my apartment. I can't leave a fourteen year old alone at this hour of the night."

"Is she your problem?" Justin asked. "Your custody?"

"No." She shook her head. "She feels safe with me."

"You're the closest thing to a parent she's got?" Martin asked.

"More like she's a tomboy and is still coming into her own, but she's not the girly-girl her mother wants. Instead of letting her find her own path, she's being pushed." She shrugged and checked her watch for another message. Thankfully, there wasn't one. "Look, I need to go. I had a great time, but this faerie princess has to go back to her regular life. Thanks for a wonderful evening. I'll never forget you." She ducked under Justin's arm and rushed into the building. She didn't bother to look back until she stood out in the parking garage next to the club. Even then, she didn't stop moving until she reached her car.

Once she slid behind the wheel, she locked the vehicle and engaged the engine. She'd learned so many things, living on her own. Never stay still for long and never be in any area where it wasn't secure. She backed out of the spot and headed home.

She should've gotten Justin or Martin's phone numbers. Should've been nicer about leaving.

Damn her sense of family and responsibility.

She'd lose out on something great because she had to help those she loved and those who drove her to the brink of insanity. Madelin needed her help.

This night would have to live in her memory.

So much for trying to find a date.

About the Author

Wendi Zwaduk is a multi-published, award-winning author of more than one-hundred short stories and novels. She's been writing since 2008 and published since 2009. Her stories range from the contemporary and paranormal to BDSM and LGBTQ themes. No matter what the length, her works are always hot, but with a lot of heart. She enjoys giving her characters a second chance at love, no matter what the form. She's been the runner up in the Kink Category at Love Romances Café as well as nominated at the LRC for best contemporary, best ménage and best anthology. Her books have made it to the bestseller lists on Amazon.com and the former AllRomance Ebooks. She also writes under the name of Megan Slayer.

When she's not writing, she spends time with her husband and son as well as three dogs and three cats. She enjoys art, music and racing, but football is her sport of choice.

Wendi loves to hear from readers. You can find her contact information, website details and author profile page at https://www.firstforromance.com

ENTWINED PUBLISHING